Hugh Scott worked as an art teacher for several years, but became a full-time writer in 1984, after winning a short story writing competition. Since then he has had fourteen books published, including his bestselling novel, *Why Weeps the Brogan?* which won the Whitbread Children's Novel Award in 1989. He is married with two grown-up children and two grandchildren, and lives in Scotland with his wife.

Other Hodder Supernatural titles available:

Look For Me By Moonlight
Mary Downing Hahn

Over the Hills and Far Away
William Mayne

Night People
Maggie Pearson

Hero
Josephine Poole

Ghost Chamber
Soul Taker
Celia Rees

Night World series
Lisa J. Smith

Companions of the Night
Vivian Vande Velde

The Blooding
Patricia Windsor

THE GRAVE-DIGGER

Hugh Scott

a division of Hodder Headline plc

First published in Great Britain in 1997
by Hodder Children's Books

10 9 8 7 6 5 4 3 2 1

A Catalogue record for this book is
available from the British Library

ISBN 0 340 68331 7

Typeset by Hewer Text Composition Services, Edinburgh
Printed and bound in Great Britain by
Mackays of Chatham, Chatham, Kent

Hodder Children's Books
a division of Hodder Headline plc
338 Euston Road
London NW1 3BH

To my wife, Margo, with buckets of love.

1

'Back in the summer of 1995,' said Grandpa. 'You remember '95, don't you, Abernetha?'

'No, Grandpa.'

'I worked in the city cemetery. You know – the graveyard . . .' Grandpa's eyebrows moved in the direction of the window.

'Yes, Grandpa,' sighed Abernetha, who had heard the story so often that she no longer listened to the words, but she did like the sound of Grandpa's voice as she curled close on his lap.

Abernetha glanced away from the coal fire to the window of Grandpa's flat, and though the curtains were drawn tight shut to keep out winter's freezing fingers, Abernetha knew that beyond the curtains, snowflakes slid down the glass, piling thick and white on the windowsill outside.

'Tell me, Grandpa,' said Abernetha, 'all about the graveyard.'

'Maybe I've told you before,' murmured Grandpa, and his hand reached past Abernetha on his lap, to the mantelpiece, where his fingers dipped into an old marmalade jar, then slid out of the jar, holding a black cigar.

Abernetha wrinkled her nose, but didn't say how strong the smell of cigar smoke was; though Grandpa had not yet lit the cigar.

'The cemetery —' mumbled Grandpa – and Abernetha knew his mumbling was caused by the cigar in his mouth, but she didn't look up; she snuggled, waiting for Grandpa to lean towards the fire for a red-hot coal.

But he didn't.

'The cemetery,' breathed Grandpa, 'in that summer of '95, needed little looking after. The weather, you see, was so hot (Did I say it was the hottest summer in three-hundred years?) and dry! the poor yew trees dropped their needles in brown thousands—'

'What are brown thousands?' piped Abernetha. She hadn't heard of *them* before!

'Thousands of brown needles. And you know that the needles are the tiny thin-as-a-pin leaves of the yew tree no longer than my old thumbnail. Oh, of course, you know that! Let me get on with my story.

'Brown thousands of needles piling up under the yew trees, and the grass brown too – why even the moss on the north side of the gravestones was dropping off and turning to dust, and during the day, ghosts shimmered above the gravestones—'

'Not real ghosts!' declared Abernetha sitting

up in Grandpa's lap and looking into his eyes. His unlit cigar waggled.

Abernetha relaxed and gazed again at the fire. 'Not real ghosts,' she told herself, because beyond the windows with the sliding snowflakes – in fact, close enough to fly a paper aeroplane onto – was the very graveyard Grandpa was talking about.

'Real ghosts,' said Grandpa. 'Oh, I know! Some people said it was warm air shimmering above the stones, because the stones were hot enough under that sun to fry an egg on—'

'Except it would run off.'

'— except it would run off. Have I told you this before?'

'No,' said Abernetha; and this was a joke between her and Grandpa: when he asked a question that he knew the answer to, Abernetha would say 'No' if she meant 'Yes', and 'Yes' if she meant 'No'.

'Very funny,' said Grandpa. He leaned forward squashing Abernetha, and his fingers held the cigar to a red-hot coal until the cigar burst with smoke and a tiny flame danced for a moment on its tip. Then Grandpa sat back, and the smoke streamed over Abernetha's head, clouding around the clock on the mantelpiece.

'Ghosts,' puffed Grandpa, 'shimmered. Now I know as well as you that ghosts live in lonely houses, or drift along deserted lanes, and you never see one yourself – it's always somebody else, or somebody else's dad, or granny, or relation now living in Australia . . .'

Abernetha wriggled impatiently as she knew she was supposed to.

'. . . not in a city,' said Grandpa.

'Not what in a city?' asked Abernetha, who had forgotten where Grandpa was in the story.

'Not ghosts in a city. It simply isn't done.

What? crowds of people seeing ghosts? It's unheard of! But – ' And more smoke clouded the clock. '– the ghosts were there, and anybody who looked could see them from the pavement. Maybe people believed the smart Alecs who said that ghosts were hot air, and—'

'Get on, Grandpa!'

'Get on. Right. Okay. It was to-oo hot to work during the day, so I would come to the graveyard early, dig a grave or two—'

'Not two,' sighed Abernetha. 'Not digging by yourself.'

'No. One grave, perhaps, and hot work it was even in the early morning. Well, one day, I did have two graves to dig – by myself . . .'

Grandpa paused, but Abernetha said nothing.

'– by myself. But two graves in the early hours of the grey dawn was more exercise than I wanted, so I waited until evening to dig the second, when the sun would be behind this tenement building—'

'Block of flats, Mummy calls it.'

'I know. But it wasn't in my young days. It was a tenement, and it hasn't changed much, so I'll call it a tenement if nobody minds. But whether it's a tenement or a block of flats, it still spread its shadow over the cemetery in the evening, letting the ground cool, oh! even the trees seemed to relax when that great cool shadow crept across them. And the ghosts – being just hot air – huh! ha! the ghosts – of course – stopped shimmering because the sun was no longer heating the gravestones.

'I must tell you, that I liked the graveyard less in the evening, because suddenly the traffic would stop. It seemed that after the rush-hour – with cars and buses shizzing past the North Gate and dust whirling in off the road and people walking around the pavement outside the cemetery railing

– it seemed that everything stopped at a quarter-past six.

'Except me, of course. I was just starting. Sitting outside my shed – tucked in behind the high bit of wall where passers-by can't see it, and the ground around the shed too full of tree roots to dig more graves in . . .'

Grandpa paused, puffing his cigar.

'You were honing your spade,' murmured Abernetha.

'Was I?'

'You were going to.'

'I believe you're right. Honing my spade with a lovely old angel's wing made of granite. The shape of the wing fitted my hand to perfection, and the broken surface – where the wing had broken off the angel – was level enough to rub across the spade's edge, sharpening it just right for cutting into the sun-hard ground.

'Well. The graveyard – by 1995 – was pretty full. One more winter, I reckoned, with old folk dying off in the cold, would see the end of my job there. No more honing my spade under the beech tree. Did I say it was a beech tree? beside my shed? Anyway. Because the graveyard was getting full, the grave I was about to dig was in the least desirable corner. D'you know what I mean? Least desirable?'

'Worst bit,' said Abernetha, who knew perfectly well what 'least desirable' meant, having heard the story hundreds of times – all her life, it seemed; and knowing also that Grandpa forgot how old she was getting. Besides, when Harry was in the mood, he told her the story too. Harry was lucky being fourteen. Really, just about grown-up.

'Are you asleep?'

'No,' sighed Abernetha. 'I was thinking about Harry.'

'He'll be home soon. Should I put you to bed?'

'I want to hear the story.'

'I want to smoke my cigar. And tell you the story.'

'It is a true story, isn't it?'

'Mm.'

'Go on then.'

'The plot that I was to dig the grave in,' said Grandpa, 'was in the least desirable part of the cemetery. You know how this tenement is as long as a street, and the cemetery is where the back gardens should be – ?'

'As long as a street.'

'Right. And around the rest of the cemetery is the cemetery wall with a high railing on top to keep the public out—'

'Or the ghosts in.'

'– or the ghosts in. Oh. You remembered. The cemetery wall (with the railing on top), circles the whole of the cemetery, with two gates for funerals to come through. The North Gate is chained shut, and trees have grown up so that y'couldn't open it even if you wanted.

Only the West Gate is used, and, of course, it is gra-and, with marbellous pillars . . .?'

Abernetha did not look up from the fire, but she could imagine Grandpa's eyebrows raised in a question waiting for her to correct him. She said, '*Marble* pillars.'

'Quite,' sighed Grandpa. 'Well. I was telling you about this least desirable plot. It is least desirable, because it is so close to the old North Gate that if the gate were to be opened, why! people would walk straight in over this grave!

'In other words, it's where the path used to be from the North Gate into the cemetery.

'But now, it is hanging with trees, and tangle-footed with weeds. Huh! weeds grow even on top of the wall between the bars of the railings – Oh! I know! I know your next question!'

'I haven't asked any questions,' said Abernetha.

'Why didn't I clear away the weeds? That was

my job? Yes, yes it was my job, but have you thought of the vast size of the cemetery? I've known grown men get lost for an afternoon. When you're in the heart of it, so overgrown are the gravestones and monuments, that you might imagine you were in a jungle . . . Vast.

'Vast is the word . . .'

'Grandpa, I know how big it is. We can see it from the windows, and I've been in it a thousand times.'

'We can. You have. You're right as usual, Abernetha.' Grandpa's hand patted Abernetha's arm as she curled up tight on his lap, and his cigar smoke drifted around her, smelling sweet and rich, like leather and Christmas cake – though strong.

'One man,' cried Grandpa, 'can't look after all that vast cemetery, all these hundreds of trees, all those thousands of gravestones. Do you know how many gravestones are out there?' Grandpa's hand left Abernetha's arm, and she knew he was pointing at the graveyard beyond the window. 'Eight thousand, nine hundred and forty-seven. Not that I've counted them, of course, but the records in the town clerk's office tell me . . . Oh, well. Never mind that. One man – as I say – can't look after such a vast place, so the weeds and trees grow thick at the North Gate, and I struck! into the weeds with my spade.

'Well. I had spent a long time rubbing the angel's wing on the spade, and maybe I'd smoked a cigar afterwards – which takes nearly an hour, and I suppose I made a mug of tea on the camping stove in the shed –

'What I'm saying is, that the sun no longer peered down on the city, so that not only was the shadow of the tenement over the graveyard, but the shadow of night was wrapping itself around the silent streets.'

Abernetha waited for the next part of Grandpa's story.

She twisted round to look up at him.

He frowned over his cigar.

'I don't like this bit,' he said. 'And I'm not sure it's suitable for little girls.'

'I've heard it before,' yawned Abernetha. 'And it didn't keep me awake. So tell me about the face, then I'll go to bed.'

2

'I dug the grave,' said Grandpa, 'sometimes watching the North Gate so that I could see cars going by.

'But that meant my back was to the cemetery and to the darkness which lay among the trees. Oh, the evening wasn't utterly dark – not black like a dustbin, you understand, for the sky swung bright as pearls beyond the city, throwing down enough light for me to work.

'Sometimes – when I'd had my back to the cemetery too long – I turned round and dug with my back to the gate.

'But then I could *see* the shadows among the

gravestones, and you know what shadows are like when you are busy, why – they change! don't they? and as your spade strikes the earth it seems that the shadows jerk as if they are alive.

'Or maybe they were just curious about my digging, for they certainly gathered closer as the sky darkened. Some people would say the shadows gathered closer *because* the sky had darkened – that is what shadows do! But shadows don't have faces.

'A few yards from where I was digging . . . Don't wriggle, Abernetha, you know perfectly well what yards are—'

'A bit less than a metre,' murmured Abernetha.

'Yes . . . was this gravestone shaped like a cross. Ho, it wasn't fat enough at all! this stone to hide anyone in the daytime, but with shovelfuls of shadow—'

'Shovelfuls of shadow,' sighed Abernetha,

enjoying the feel of Grandpa's words in her mouth.

'– heaped behind the cross, why several people could have crouched out of sight.

'Then I saw the face peeping over the cross. And I kept my head up out of the grave (for I had dug deep down by this time) and stared; but I saw that the face was simply leaves catching a trickle of light from the sky.

'So I dug again, throwing earth up onto the ground. I had to look again at the leaves to make sure they were just leaves, but maybe the light had changed, because now I couldn't see them; though nearer the ground, peeping from behind the cross, was another face.

'Or the same face.

'Well. Your old Grandpa was used to ghosts and shadows, and I didn't bother climbing out of the grave to see who was there. If anybody! Huh! Who would sneak about in a graveyard at that time of night?

'Well. I tidied the bottom of the grave and left a shiny five-pence piece for luck, like I always do, for the coffin to lie on, and pulled myself up onto the ground.

'I sat on the heap of earth I'd dug out, and wiped sweat from my brow with my handkerchief, and I saw the face still staring at me.

'"Leaves," I told myself. I'd seen faces in leaves a thousand times. Why did this face trouble me?

'The answer was that the eyes shone like real eyes in the dusk, and I swore they blinked – though I moved my head at that second, so maybe the light had simply ducked off the leaves so that the eyes only seemed to blink.

'I was suddenly fed up with myself. I stuck my spade in the heap of earth and marched towards the cross.

'The eyes watched me.

'I stood, why – a coffin's length from the cross – staring down while the eyes stared up.

'"You're not real," I said out loud, and took two steps closer, crouched, and reached out my hand.'

‡

'My fingers,' said Grandpa, 'grasped weeds growing at the base of the cross.

'There was no face. So I stepped back trying to make out a face again, in the weeds; but I couldn't. Maybe grabbing the weeds had changed their shape too much. The odd thing was, these weeds had no leaves – just stalks and seed heads—'

'Grass,' whispered Abernetha, wakening up.

'Quite. Grass. So I fetched my spade, thinking about grass. Artificial grass – in fact – to place on the ground around the grave to make it pleasant for tomorrow's mourners.

'I fetched my spade. I said that, didn't I? Pulled it out of the pile of earth, and something in the grave caught my eye.

'For a second, I thought it was the coin I'd

left. But I realised that the tiny shine was not in the middle of the grave where the coin was, but at the end where a face might be if someone was lying there.

'Then a second tiny shine appeared beside the first, like eyes, watching me, and I leaned down, the spade in my hands, wishing I had a match, because I knew I had used my last match on my cigar.

'Then I decided to be angry.

'If some so-and-so was playing silly-pumpkins, trying to scare a man at his work – me, I mean – well, he would jolly well find out he'd chosen the wrong man. I raised the spade—

'The spade – as you have seen often enough, Abernetha – is a grave-digger's spade, or trenching spade, with a long, long handle for reaching into the grave, so I knew I could strike the so-and-so at the bottom of the grave – for I believed someone really was lying down there looking up at me.

'Anyway, I raised the spade, and growled, "Come out you so-and-so." (Though I may not have used the words "so-and-so".) Then I raised the spade higher, slowly, knowing that whoever was in the grave would see it raised in the last glimmer of evening light.

'"Out!" I shouted, and I swung the spade down reaching right to the bottom of the grave.

'Now. I didn't swing it hard. I knew what I was doing. I didn't want to cut somebody in half – because I'd honed the edge sharp remember.

'Well. The eyes vanished as if they'd shut, and I felt... Well, I felt as if I'd taught the so-and-so a lesson, and I expected a gasp, but no gasp puffed out of the grave.

'The spade touched the earth, and I stared; and I saw the glint of my five-pence piece again – as if it had just been uncovered

– as if, I told myself, somebody had been lying on it, but somehow that someone had jumped up and escaped, even as I swung my spade.'

3

Abernetha woke up in bed, and saw bright light through her closed eyelids. She felt her duvet over her, and prodded her toes into it. She lay quietly, remembering Grandpa's story, and remembering she had slept through some of it.

She also remembered Grandpa's cigary kiss on her brow as he tucked her into bed.

She opened her eyes.

The bedroom walls stood bright with winter light. Abernetha heaved the duvet aside, and ran to the window. Someone strode past outside, ghost-footed in the snow. Traffic moved as if in whispers, because snow silenced the roll of tyres.

Abernetha got dressed, noticing that Harry's bed had not been slept in. She had hoped he'd come in after she was asleep, but maybe he wasn't well enough yet to get out of hospital, and, oh, well, snow is top-of-the-class! thought Abernetha as she fled to the kitchen where cereal waited to crackle, and hot chocolate simmered on the cooker not daring to boil over with Grandpa's eye on it.

'Then what happened?' asked Abernetha, thinking of the story.

'Kiss.' Grandpa pointed at his face and Abernetha dragged herself around the kitchen table and kissed him.

Then she ate her cereal, waiting.

'D'you really want the rest of the story?' Grandpa asked the hot chocolate.

'No,' said Abernetha.

Grandpa sighed.

He said, 'I didn't put the artificial grass around the grave. I mentioned the artificial grass, didn't I? It was dark, you see, and I suppose I got a fright – though not much, being your Grandpa and . . .'

'. . . very brave.'

'Mm. Now. I have said, that the cemetery had two entrances.'

'Yes.'

'And only the West Gate was used.'

Crunch! crunched Abernetha on her cereal.

'And the West Gate is furthest from this tenement, and leaving by that gate I would have to walk a-all round the road round the cemetery to get home.'

Abernetha frowned. She thought, . . . all round the road round the cemetery. I like that.

'And this tenement,' said Grandpa, 'has no doors out the back because they would take you among the gravestones. But—'

Abernetha, as she crunched, glanced at the kitchen window with snow on its sill, and beyond, gravestones padded white.

'—that very window wasn't locked. Leaving it unlocked while I dug graves seemed a good idea – so that I could cut through the cemetery, pull the window open and step through it into our kitchen – this kitchen.

'Ready for your chocolate?' Grandpa zoomed the chocolate in its pan, to the table, and poured it into Abernetha's mug.

'After seeing the whatever-it-was in the grave, I hurried through the cemetery, leaving my five-pence piece on guard.

'Remember how dark it was that night? And no lights on in the cemetery. There are one or two lamp posts now, with bulbs that work, but none then; though in this tenement, lights shone out, but they simply made yellow squares in what seemed the night sky, brightening the cemetery not-at-all so that the darkness lay like black fog. If you know this trick – ' and Grandpa poured himself some chocolate and lit a cigar. He snapped his fingers. Snapping was the trick. '– you can hear if you are close to a tree because the sound comes back like a ball bouncing off a wall. It doesn't take much practice to know the sound of a yew with its soft mass of needles (those that haven't lost their brown thousands), from the sound of a beech with its fat bare trunk; and the gravestones give back a smaller echo, I'd say.'

'You're making that up,' said Abernetha.

'Really? So I hurried in the dark (after seeing the whatever-it-was), snapping (or not snapping if you don't believe me), and not looking back, for only darkness followed me; then I fumbled at the window, got it open, stepped in here onto the linoleum and clicked the window shut, laid the spade in the corner by the fireplace which was packed with summer flowers. I closed the curtains, switched on the light, told myself I had imagined the face, ate my supper, set my alarm—'

'You're rushing,' warned Abernetha.

'I was in a hurry,' protested Grandpa. 'Went to bed—'

'Cleaned your teeth.'

'Cleaned my teeth, went to bed, slept, got up, ate breakfast as dawn came rubbing at the window, grabbed the spade and hurried more slowly back to my shed for the artificial grass, then even more slo-owly, returned to the grave where I had seen the eyes looking up at me. Toast?'

'Little bit. When will Harry come?'

'Lunch time, I expect. You know how that boy can eat.'

'Keeps his strength up, he says,' said Abernetha. 'Harry's stronger than any boy in his school. Is he hurt badly?'

'And stronger than any teacher. Takes after his Grandpa,' said Grandpa peering under the grill at the toast and blowing cigar smoke across the cooker.

'Mm,' said Abernetha. 'I'm going out to play.'

'Are you? What about the story? I don't know if he's hurt badly. You still want toast?'

'All right.'

'Toast, it is,' said Grandpa dancing the hot toast on his palm across to Abernetha. 'Butter. Marmalade. Shall I spread it?'

He spread it, his cigar leaking smoke towards the ceiling.

'Finish the story, then,' ordered Abernetha.

'Oh, there's little more. When I got to the grave – carrying the artificial grass over my shoulder – someone had filled it in.'

4

Abernetha knew that someone had filled in the grave. Hadn't she heard the story hundreds of times?

But she still was thrilled, her shoulders cuddling up towards her ears.

And 1995 was another of her jokes with Grandpa, for it was still 1995 now, and the summer just past was the hottest summer in three hundred years.

And Abernetha frowned, for wasn't she telling herself she had heard the story hundreds of times, all her life? and that wasn't true – four times, maybe, she'd heard it, since the summer

– and once from Harry. Though it *felt* true. She wondered if things could be true and not true at the same time.

Then she told herself not to be silly, and finished her toast, suffered another smoky kiss on her brow, and safe in her wellingtons, and in her anorak with its hood up, she opened the kitchen window and dropped out into the snow.

She heard the window shut behind her, and knew Grandpa was watching her high-stepping through a snowdrift against the tenement wall. But she forgot Grandpa and rolled a snowball around, leaving a bare trail as the ball gathered a snowman's body from the ground.

The snowball, when it was as tall as Abernetha's knees refused to be pushed; she began another ball and rolled it; but it broke and sulkily stayed broken no matter how Abernetha persuaded it to stick together.

'I didn't really want a snowman,' said

Abernetha to the broken snow. 'You would have been his head, but what use is a silly broken head? – which you're not going to be. Actually, I'm not a girl; I am an Arctic explorer and I think I'll do some exploring.' And she trudged off in her wellingtons between the gravestones, into the bright white winter light of the vast cemetery.

She looked back, and Grandpa waved from the window, his eyes steady through his cigar smoke.

Abernetha glanced down at her footprints, then turned and marched on.

She would take the route travelled only once before by her long-dead grandpa – the greatest explorer of all time – who had once dug a grave in which to bury his huskies, who had died of measles.

Now that *was* silly.

Frostbite would be better, decided Abernetha.

Anyway, whatever they died of, she was going to look at their grave.

So she walked on, stopping only to throw hand-grenades at polar bears. The grenades exploded beautifully against the trees and vanished, for they were special white grenades which blended with the environment and burst with almost no noise.

After a long walk, she found a ship frozen in the ice and rubbed snow from the slab of stone which was the deck, and found that someone had died in this ship in 1788. 'But this is the wrong grave!' wailed Abernetha. 'Shall I ever find the burial place of dear dead Grandpa's faithful huskies?

'Oh, there it is.'

Abernetha stood still, looking towards the North Gate.

She was surprised she had come so far already. Her anorak cuffs made cold wet circles around her wrists. Why, she must have walked across this vast cemetery almost without noticing!

Abernetha recognised the grave that Grandpa had dug, because he had shown it to her before, and there it was again, as close to the North Gate as the trees would allow, with its headstone wearing a thick white hat.

And someone was standing beside the grave.

‡

Someone familiar, thought Abernetha, but so wrapped up in winter clothes that she wasn't sure . . .

A snowflake descended out of the grey sky.

Abernetha smiled as the flake wobbled onto the white ground. If the snow fell heavily, school would be closed tomorrow, and she would have Harry to herself when Mum brought him home. He probably had a twisted ankle. Or something not too bad, but bad enough to stop him doing the Adventure Course.

More flakes floated down; and Abernetha saw that the person at the grave wasn't looking at the gravestone, but had his hand raised as if waiting for Abernetha to notice him. But the snow flurried thick suddenly, dissolving the man –

Or was it a boy?

– dissolving him as if God had rubbed him out with a snowy rubber.

'How desirably curious,' said Abernetha. She stepped forward, but stumbled a little in the snow, and glanced at her wellingtons; her glance only took a moment, but when she looked up, the man –

Or boy.

– was gone.

'Rubbed right out,' thought Abernetha, stumping forward until she reached the grave.

'Gone somewhere,' she told the North Gate, 'though which way . . .'

She shivered, her spine cold; colder than it should have been, she knew, even on this wintery day.

And she stared through the flakes in every direction, but saw only trees drooping, their arms tired of carrying parcels of snow.

Abernetha raised her eyebrows. What did it matter where the boy had gone? (She had decided it was a boy.)

She blinked as snowflakes made their home on her lashes. She wiped her eyes and pushed back her anorak hood, and she could hear the silence of the cemetery, and the soundless rushing-down of the lovely snow, and she could see her wellington prints smoothed out now by the new flakes, though still visible.

Abernetha looked for the boy's footprints. They – of course! – would tell her which direction the boy had taken; though come to think of it, he would head for the West Gate, wouldn't he? It's the only way out; unless he was heading for some window in the tenement. The block of flats.

The tenement.

She liked 'tenement' better.

'What *was* I thinking about?' asked Abernetha. 'I know. The boy's footprints.'

She looked around, but could see only her own, fading fast.

'He was standing here,' Abernetha reminded herself, 'right where I am. Oh, maybe I've scuffed his footprints away. But where are the footprints he left, when he left?

'The snow looks not walked-on to me.'

As Abernetha turned slowly, her fingers touching the top of the gravestone for balance – through its snowy cap – the cold on her spine jangled thrillingly into her stomach, because no matter which way she turned, she could see no boy's footprints.

And she felt how far she was from the kitchen window where Grandpa had waved to her, and how still the trees stood, as if they were thinking of stepping closer; and how cold and hard the gravestones seemed, as if they had got colder and harder to resist the snow, and how, and how! the snow swirled down faster so that further-off trees vanished and a cold crust of flakes clung to Abernetha's cheek—

Then she knew who the boy was. She knew, because of the way he had stood with his hand raised.

It was Harry, her big brother.

5

'Harry!' protested Abernetha.

She smiled. Harry had come home and was playing a trick. 'Harry! Harry! Harry!' She ran through the falling snow, then stopped. 'Harry!'

She couldn't see him.

She ran another way, among the trees which blocked the North Gate and grabbed the bars of the gate, her fingers breaking the snow that had gathered on the bars. She said, 'Harry?' but he wasn't outside on the pavement. He wasn't on the farther pavement with cars moving carefully between him and Abernetha.

'And how *could* he be there!' Abernetha scolded herself, 'with the gate chained shut!' So she dashed again, thinking of heading to the West Gate, but she stopped, for she knew that Harry wouldn't be so cruel as to go that far.

So she walked back towards the grave which appeared out of the snow storm (she noticed she was now walking in a snow storm, though it was not a noisy storm; it was a silent thick dropping storm); and at the grave she could not find even her own footprints which would lead her back to Grandpa.

She wondered if Harry had become cruel – hiding for so long. Abernetha ignored a warm snowflake that got in her eye, for Arctic explorers don't cry in case their tears freeze, blinding them. So she walked away from the grave towards home, with no footprints to lead her, pretending not to care that Harry was cruel.

*   *   *

Abernetha flumped along, her boots dragging in the snow, her face tucked down to prevent tears escaping onto her cheeks; a gravestone popped up in front of her, and she grunted at it, and walked round, and trudged on, wondering why Harry was being mean.

Fancy! going away on a course then getting taken to hospital and Mum having to dash off to hold his hand, then coming back like *that!* hiding in the snow and not leaving footprints! It was a bit much! And not jumping out to grab her.

It wasn't like Harry to be mean.

Or not to leave footprints.

Humph.

Maybe it wasn't Harry, after all.

After all, he'd been wrapped up in so many clothes it could have been anybody. Even a girl. Though the raised hand wasn't a girl's gesture. It was a boy's gesture. It was Harry's—

'Sorry,' mumbled Abernetha to a tree she had bumped into.

She put her sad mood away at the back of her mind, and peered through the snow. She said, 'Harry?' hoping now he wouldn't answer because she wanted to be unforgiving.

And he didn't answer; so Abernetha held up her proud face and walked on, snow on her lashes, not sure where she was going, because the trees wore white fur coats instead of green summer leaves, which made everywhere look different. Why! here was a beech tree, and Abernetha knew every beech tree in the cemetery, but this one might have been in disguise. She rubbed snow from the trunk, and shook a branch sending snow springing off, but the tree held itself too high in the storm for Abernetha to make out its arms; it was by their arms that she recognised the beech trees, because they all had beautiful arms with smooth silvery-grey skin over plump muscles.

'Which is all very well if only I could see them!' she complained to the tree. 'But you're hiding just like Harry's hiding! And I wish you wouldn't, because I'm getting cold, and my wrists are wet and sore, but I don't suppose you care! Well, just see if I picnic under you this spring! because I won't!'

And Abernetha, prouder than ever, ran away across the deep white ground.

Then she stopped running, and walked, forgetting her pride, and found a gravestone to lean against, because she was tired with lifting her feet high through the snow, and because she really didn't know which way to go.

She panted, and wondered if she should cry. She wasn't lost exactly; she knew she was between the North Gate and home; she just couldn't tell if home was straight ahead, or to the left . . .

She decided that her tears should be let loose about now. Then she thought that maybe that's what Harry was waiting for, now he was cruel; and he would pop out and laugh at her tears.

'Explorers,' Abernetha reminded herself, 'don't have tears freezing their eyes up.' And she walked on until a small tree approached her with its arms out – then she stopped.

But the tree still approached.

It said, 'Abernetha?' in Grandpa's voice, and Abernetha stood still while the tree turned completely into Grandpa, and his arms clasped her and lifted her so that her face went into his damp scarf, and the bristles of his cheek jagged her cheek; but she didn't move to make herself comfortable; she lay still in Grandpa's arms, saying nothing, while Grandpa said, 'I thought you might like some company. And I thought I might like a walk in the snow. So here we are together. Aren't the trees beautiful! I sometimes wish I could paint, and I would paint the cemetery with blobs of white for the snow, and strokes of grey for the beech trees . . .'

Grandpa talked, and Abernetha's face bounced deeper into his scarf, and she forgot about his bristles against her cheeks, and she felt warmer, and thought only about getting into the kitchen where the fire would dry her sore wrists and she could sit in Grandpa's chair with cushions around her . . .

Grandpa's boots squeaked on linoleum, and Abernetha raised her head to the warmth of the kitchen. Grandpa stood her on the rug while he shut the window.

Then he carried her by the elbows close to the fire and pulled off her anorak; pushed her into his chair, pulled off her wellingtons, plucked off her socks which clung only to her toes she discovered; and her feet were wet with snow that had sneaked higher than her wellingtons and had popped down for a warm.

Then Grandpa helped her off with her

trousers and wrapped her in her dressing gown, and packed cushions around her.

Then a pot clanged on the stove and a hot chocolate smell sweetened the air, so that Abernetha felt cheerier, and smiled at Grandpa.

He smiled back, but his smile was not the one Abernetha expected.

It was a smile pretending to be happier than it was.

6

Grandpa sat in front of the fire on a low stool and sipped his chocolate. Abernetha put her bare feet on his knee, and she sipped her chocolate, watching Grandpa's face.

She hadn't said anything since Grandpa had picked her up in the snow. She wanted very much to say that she had seen Harry, but she didn't; she knew she shouldn't.

So she watched Grandpa's face.

Grandpa sipped, and gulped. He blinked into the fire. He said, 'Your Mum phoned from the hospital.'

Abernetha watched as Grandpa's lips touched his mug; but he didn't drink.

'She took Harry,' said Grandpa, 'as you know, to the Adventure Camp. Winter conditions, Abernetha. Good for young men of Harry's ability. He... um... fell. As you know. Yesterday, and went into Central Hospital.'

Grandpa's eyes turned on Abernetha, and she stared back. She shook her head. She had seen him. Maybe. 'He's not dead,' she told Grandpa.

'No,' agreed Grandpa. 'He's not dead.'

'Do you mean he's not dead yet?'

Grandpa raised his eyebrows then pulled them down in a mighty frown. He gulped his hot chocolate.

'Maybe,' he whispered.

Abernetha glared at her toes on Grandpa's knee. It seemed the sensible thing to do.

She pulled her shoulders up close to her ears.

She said, 'I saw him.'

Grandpa said, 'When your Mum phoned, I thought I should come out to find you. Besides the snow, of course. You saw him? You saw someone in the cemetery?'

'Harry. He was at that grave. He raised his hand to me. I think he was wearing his new anorak.'

'Well now.'

Grandpa sat straight-backed on the stool. 'There's a thing,' he breathed, and Abernetha knew he didn't believe her.

She said, 'Can we go and see him? At the hospital, I mean.'

'No, no. Just Mum, today. She'll tell us what's what. My goodness! but you were out for a long time! Exploring were you? Polar bears—!'

'I did see Harry,' insisted Abernetha.

Grandpa's hand rested on Abernetha's feet.

She wriggled her toes under his warm palm.

She said, 'Tell me the rest of the story, Grandpa. Somebody filled in the grave.' Abernetha's voice trembled. 'You always stop there!'

'All right, all right. Try not to worry, Abernetha. The doctors are very, very good at the Central.'

'I don't care! Harry was mean to me! He waved, then he hid and never jumped out at me . . .' A sob caught Abernetha by surprise.

Grandpa hurriedly lowered his mug onto the hearth and knelt beside Abernetha, one hand behind her head, the other patting her fingers. 'There, there,' he said. 'There, there, Abernetha. Harry's a strong boy. And with good doctoring . . .'

'Why was he mean?' she wept.

'It wasn't Harry, sweetheart. Just some boy playing a trick. I'll get you a hanky.'

Abernetha cried, then a hanky arrived at her nose and she blew and she drank her chocolate, and felt better, waiting for the story.

'Oh, the story,' said Grandpa, settling on his stool. 'Well. I haven't told you the rest of it, because I don't like speaking ill of people – thinking bad thoughts, Abernetha, can be dangerous.'

Grandpa frowned into the fire.

Abernetha wondered what could be dangerous about thinking bad thoughts. Then she wanted to know who Grandpa was going to speak ill of.

'Who do you mean?' she asked.

'When I found the grave filled in,' said Grandpa slowly, 'I had some words to say, I can tell you.

'But since the person who had filled the grave in wasn't around, I said the words to myself and to the iron bars of the North Gate. The trees – of course – covered their ears. Then I remembered there were people sleeping all round me—'

'Under the ground,' smiled Abernetha through her damp eyes, because she hadn't heard this joke before.

'Under the ground. So I stopped saying things, and went back to my shed for the spade and I shovelled, and shovelled, and shovelled, and . . .'

As Grandpa said, 'shovelled' he sank lower and lower on his stool until he nearly toppled into the fire, and Abernetha shrieked and would have spilled her chocolate if her mug hadn't been empty. Then Grandpa was properly on the stool again and saying, 'Of course, shovelling the loose earth out of the grave wasn't hard work – and when I got to the bottom I looked for my five-pence piece. But I couldn't find it. I couldn't find it at the top of the pile of earth either, though I fingered through it carefully.

'Then I laid the artificial grass neatly on the ground around the grave and let it hang down a little way into the grave, and draped another piece of grass over the heap of earth – to make things pleasant, you see, for the mourners who would arrive at eleven o'clock that morning.'

'But didn't you—?'

'Certainly, I did,' Grandpa assured Abernetha. 'I stood and scratched my head wondering who had filled in my grave, and why anyone would take such trouble. I mean, it did no one any good that I could fathom. And my spade had been clean when I fetched it from my shed, so if someone *had* used it, then they must have cleaned it, and left it locked inside the shed again, hanging between the nails on the wall. And the problem with that is, how did whoever-did-the-digging unlock the shed door?'

'Maybe he brought his own spade,' said Abernetha, and she shivered and clutched a cushion to her chest, for the snow had chilled her more than she'd realised. She whispered, 'Or maybe you forgot to lock the shed.'

Grandpa glanced at her, then rattled coal from the brass coal-scuttle onto the fire, and puffed air into the fire with bellows. 'I'll turn the central heating up, too,' he said, and creaked off his stool, then he returned, and the central heating thudded distantly for a minute until Abernetha forgot about it.

'There was this woman,' said Grandpa, 'among the mourners. She wasn't dressed in black, and she had no black arm band to show she was mourning.

'She was angry – though she never spoke.

'I stand back, you understand, from a funeral, under a tree, until everyone has gone, then I fill in the grave – which is how I see the people. That woman surely caught my attention. Oh, I remember. She tapped her foot. Tap, tap, tap on the dry earth, until her shoe was brown with dust. And her mouth was tight shut to keep it from saying things she would regret. Not old, she wasn't, and not young, but good-looking. You know,' said Grandpa.

'She didn't go off with the others when the funeral service was over. Everybody shook hands with the minister, but *he* had to approach *her*, then he left, and she stayed.

'And she said something I couldn't catch, but nobody was there except the deceased – the dead person. That was a woman too. She was talking into the grave at the dead woman.

'Then she saw me.

'I was startled when she marched towards me, and I looked round to see if someone else was waiting behind me, but there was only me; and right close she came and looked up into my face, and she was *good-looking*! And she said, "Don't fill it in!" Just like that. Fierce but quiet. And not crazy. "Do you hear me?" she hissed, for I was that startled, I'd said nothing.

'And I nodded – meaning I'd heard her; then

I shook my head, and said, "I've got to fill it in. It's my job." And she opened her handbag, and I said, "No, no, no, no, no . . ."

'I couldn't accept money, but she pushed a funny brown five pound note into my hand, and hissed at me so that I stood straighter to get my face away from hers: "Don't fill it in yet!"

'Then she marched away towards the West Gate.

'Then I looked at the note in my hand wondering what to do, because I couldn't accept it, and I couldn't go chasing a woman through the graveyard waving money at her; then I saw it wasn't a five pound note – it was a fifty pound note.'

'Fifty,' said Abernetha. 'What did you do then?'

'I didn't know what to do, and that's the truth. I stood where I was, wondering.

'I knew I couldn't keep the fifty pounds. I'd

give that to my supervisor at the town hall. My problem was, should I take the fifty pounds now, to the supervisor, or fill in the grave first? I suppose I didn't want somebody to come up and say I'd accepted money from the woman, which would get me into trouble – though who could do that, I didn't know, because nobody was about.

'Then I realised that doing my job came first. I couldn't go to the town hall, leaving the coffin uncovered in the grave.

'I felt better having made that decision, and lifted my spade from behind the tree I was standing under, when the branches shook above my head, and leaves rattled, and down came something through the leaves, and landed at my feet, laughing nastily.'

7

'Oh, I know,' sighed Abernetha. She handed Grandpa her empty mug, and he put it on the hearth.

'Warmer now, are you?' he asked. 'What do you know?'

'Angry Agatha,' said Abernetha patting the cushion from her chest onto her lap. 'Yes, I'm warm, thank you.'

'Her name,' said Grandpa, 'is Jennifer Antrim, and yes, it was her. She'd been spying. Why d'you call her Angry Agatha?'

'Because she makes people angry. What did she want? She always wants something.'

'She wanted the fifty pounds,' sighed Grandpa. 'Some kids have no honour these days. She wanted the fifty pounds or she'd tell somebody at the town hall that I had accepted it . . . How she knew to report me to the town hall, I can't imagine . . .'

'She always knows that sort of thing, Grandpa,' said Abernetha. 'She knows where all our teachers live, and the names of everybody in their families. She's horrible. Shall I give you a cigar? I can reach.'

Abernetha stretched from among her cushions and snatched a cigar from the marmalade jar and Grandpa said, 'Thank you,' and prodded it into the fire until it puffed with smoke.

'Did you slap her?' asked Abernetha, smelling the leather and Christmas cake taste of the cigar.

'I felt like it. But I didn't. I helped her to her feet, and she jerked her arm away and said she'd tell the police I'd touched her. So I put my spade over my shoulder and walked from under the tree towards the grave. Some people are just trouble from the soles of their feet to the tops of their mean little heads. I heard her following me. I shovelled in my first spadeful of earth—'

'Shovelful,' corrected Abernetha.

Grandpa narrowed one eye.

'Jennifer Antrim said,' continued Grandpa, '"Give me that money, old man, or I'll get you into big trouble."

'I went on shovelling.

'The earth lands with a hollow sound, Abernetha, when it hits the coffin, then it lands more solidly as the coffin is covered. I said, "One day, little girl, you'll be down in a grave, and God will expect you to explain your nastiness to Him."

'D'you know what she said?

'She said she wasn't nasty, and she'd tell

her father that I was saying bad things about her.

'I felt sorry for her then. She meant it, you know, Abernetha. She really didn't know she was nasty. Oh, she knew she annoyed people, but she thought – I think – that everybody behaved like that.'

'Everybody does behave like that – to her,' said Abernetha. 'Poor little thing.'

Grandpa looked at Abernetha, and Abernetha said, 'What?'

'I thought you didn't like her?' said Grandpa.

'I don't. I told you, Grandpa, she's horrible. What did she say next?'

'Oh. Yes. The poor little thing went on accusing me of everything from spitting on the coffin, to murdering old Miss Broom – that was the lady in the coffin. I told her to go away, but she only sat on my heap of earth daring me to cut her with my spade then she'd sue me. Then

– while I was trying to think how to get rid of her – for I don't understand people who tell lies – she started on about murder again.

'I shovelled earth from under her until she was forced to get out of my way. And she shrieked that I had buried Miss Broom alive and wouldn't I like to know who had filled in the grave.

'That stopped me shovelling.

'I stared at her. Her little thin face was shrivelled with thin thoughts. She was full of pride because she'd caught my attention. I suppose she didn't know she could've caught my attention more easily by being pleasant. But bursting with pride and silliness she was, her eyes skrinkled until her skin was like knitted bags around two wet raisins. Poor little thing.

'"Well," she sneered, "want to know now, don't you, old man?"

'And I knew that if I showed any interest she'd

shut up about it. So I went on shovelling, and sure enough, she couldn't keep it to herself.

'"I was hiding up a tree!" she said – as if that was a pinnacle of childhood achievement.'

Grandpa puffed Christmas cake smoke around the clock on the mantelpiece. He squinted at Abernetha. 'You know what I mean?' he asked. 'A pinnacle of childhood achievement?'

'Yes,' said Abernetha, because she didn't know what it meant.

'It means, reaching the top of something worthwhile. Doing something that's really good to do. Accomplishing—'

'Get on, Grandpa!' chided Abernetha. 'Angry Agatha always thinks that sneaking is clever. What next?'

'What next is,' said Grandpa, 'that I went on throwing earth into that grave as if I didn't care what the child had to say. She wandered off a little way and sat under one of the trees that block the North Gate. I never looked directly at her, but I saw her well enough as I slid the spade into the earth and turned to drop it with a thud! down into the grave. Funny how the sound is muffled down in a hole.

'But Jennifer was hitting the ground with her heel, saying, "Got you!" then again, "Got you! I don't like ants," she said; and I went on shovelling, and she went on saying, "Got you!" Though whether she was really killing ants—'

'I expect she was,' said Abernetha.

'– or trying to provoke me into scolding her, I couldn't tell, but I shut my ears to her wickedness, and eventually she stopped, and I eased my back, but never caught her eye; and people hurried past beyond the gate, and traffic droned on the road outside the cemetery; then she said, "I did see who filled in the grave."

'I said, "Did you." Not a question. I was being polite. A school teacher once told me she was always polite to children because they were people, just like grown-ups were people—'

'Grandpa,' warned Abernetha.

'Right, right,' said Grandpa, sucking his cigar. 'Poor Jennifer Antrim. You understand why I'm saying poor Jennifer? Because she is an unhappy child. She doesn't realise, Abernetha, that there is a better way to view the world—'

'Grandpa! What did she tell you?'

'She told me that she really was hiding in a tree the night before, watching me dig the grave. She'd seen me searching behind the stone cross, though – of course – she didn't know that I was looking for a face. She said I was a stupid old man, creeping about after shadows! She wasn't afraid of shadows!

'"Why, old man," she sneered, "I watched a shadow after you'd gone. Slipping among the gravestones!" And she pointed towards the West Gate where a visitor would come in. "It must've slid out of a tomb, and probably did, because it might have been a ghost, and probably was; in fact, it definitely was! because its feet didn't make a noise, and it slipped into your hut, old man, as if you hadn't locked the door, and brought out your shovel—"'

'Spade.'

'She called it a shovel,' said Grandpa. '"– and shovelled the earth back in, panting and groaning horribly all the time. Then it wiped the shovel with a hanky and put it back in the hut and slipped away again and I've got the very hanky because it left it beside the grave, so there!"

'Well. I almost looked at her.

'I wasn't taken in by that ghost nonsense; anybody walking among the gravestones instead of on the path would be walking on grass and therefore quiet; but when she mentioned the hanky – well! As I say, I almost looked at her.

'But I'd eased my back long enough, and I began throwing earth into the grave again, and she waved something which caught my eye, and I did look at her. She held out a hanky.

'"Very interesting," I said, and went on shovelling.

'She walked closer, determined to catch my attention.

'"It's a ghost's hanky!" she shouted.

'"Really. Got runny noses, have they?"'

'Oh, Grandpa.'

'I did think she'd walk off in a huff then, but I talked on as if I'd meant to say this sooner: "I expect you're right, Jennifer. If ghosts have noses, they probably run, same as everybody else's." And she relaxed, and held the handkerchief close to my hand.

'I looked at her again.

'She really is a pathetic little thing. I pushed the spade into the last of the heap of earth, and took the handkerchief from her. I said, "Thank you."

'"Thank you," she repeated – not thanking

me, you understand, just repeating it, as if no one had ever thanked her before.

'The handkerchief was a lady's handkerchief. Very soft. Good quality, I'd say, though I know nothing about ladies, or their handkerchiefs, of course. It was dirty with earth, and the dirt rubbed in as if someone had wiped a spade with it, right enough. The initial R was embroidered into one corner.

'"Groaning, was she?" I asked Jennifer, pretending not to care.

'"I wasn't scared!"

'"I groan sometimes," I told her, "when I'm digging, if the ground's wet; rain makes the soil heavy, and bending squeezes a groan out of me. Occasionally."

'"The ghost was crying," she said.

'"Crying? I've never done that." I let her take the handkerchief from me. She wandered off again, but she wasn't trying to get one over on me this time – she was trying to decide something.

'Then she turned, and her face wasn't so ugly, because she wasn't thinking about herself. She said, "I think it was that lady who gave you the money." She looked at her feet. "Not really a ghost."

'"I see."

'Then Jennifer did wander off. She looked back, and called, "Thank you," as if she'd never used the words before. Then she yelled, "Old man!" and ran away cackling, mean as ever. I'd better start thinking about lunch.'

8

'I wonder,' said Grandpa, his head and his cigar inside the larder, 'how Jennifer knew it was old Miss Broom getting buried. Scotch pie? Beans and pork sausage?'

'I told you, Grandpa, she knows everything that's not her business. Beans and sausage.'

'Please.'

'Please, darling Grandpa.'

'No need to overdo it.'

Grandpa went frowning to the tin-opener with the tin of beans and pork sausage.

Abernetha said, 'Couldn't she have read Miss Broom's name on the gravestone?'

'The stone wasn't in place then. I put it in later.'

'And did you take the fifty pounds to your supervisor?'

'No...oo.'

'No?' demanded Abernetha, and Grandpa smiled, so she knew he would tell her eventually. She said, 'Did you see the good-looking lady again?'

'Yes.'

'You liked her.'

'Oh, yes.'

'Did Mum mind? Does she mind?'

'Well, your mum knows better than to mind. I'm not too old, Abernetha, for ladies to look twice at me. I keep myself fit, and I've always been strong. You know that. Any grey in my hair?

'A little.'

'There you are then.'

'So you do fancy her,' decided Abernetha.

The phone rang in the hall, and Grandpa almost dropped the tin-opener. He darted away, and Abernetha heard, 'Is he all right?' and she remembered Harry lying hurt in hospital.

She clambered out from her cushions and tiptoed into the hall and stood listening, watching Grandpa's anxious face.

'Pyjamas,' said Grandpa. 'Sponge. Toothbrush. He can brush his teeth? Oh. Later maybe. Mary, Mary, don't cry. The doctors will look after him. Have you had any breakfast? You must. I was just going to feed your daughter . . . It's lunch time. Okay. You eat too. See you soon. Everything will be all right.'

Grandpa hung up the phone and looked at Abernetha. 'Harry's not any worse.'

'Is he going to die?'

'I don't know. We've to take some things to the hospital. Can you find dry clothes for yourself, Abernetha? Are you warm enough to go back out? That's a good girl. I'll get ready.'

Abernetha returned to the kitchen and put the fireguard against the fire to keep its sparks off the rug. She looked at her tin of beans and pork sausage, then went to rummage for dry clothes.

✣

Doctors in white coats. Nurses smiling. Abernetha thought there were lots of curtains in the hospital. She followed Grandpa and a nurse into a ward, and found Mum beside a bed, and in the bed a metal cage with Harry's face inside it, and his eyes shut as if they would never open again.

Mum hugged Abernetha, and Grandpa held Mum's hand, and asked if she'd eaten.

'Talk to him,' said Mum to Abernetha, nodding at Harry in the cage.

'Why is he in a cage?' asked Abernetha.

'He's hurt his neck; to keep him from moving it.'

'Will he hear me?'

Grandpa said, 'Talk to him, Abernetha, while I take your mum for a sandwich. You can't not eat, Mary,' urged Grandpa, and he took Mum away.

'Harry?' said Abernetha. 'Are you there? I tried to build a snowman this morning. And I nearly got lost in a snow storm in the cemetery. Grandpa's been telling me the story of the grave getting filled in, and he told me about Angry Agatha – you know – Jennifer Antrim who sneaks and knows things about everybody. He hadn't told me about her before, because he didn't want to speak ill of her. What happened to your neck?'

Harry drew in a shuddery breath and his lips opened.

'You can tell me,' said Abernetha. 'Nobody will mind if it was your fault. You didn't do much of the adventure course, did you? Just arrived, now here you are in hospital. How did you fall?'

Harry's lips closed.

Abernetha looked around.

She sighed. It was difficult talking to someone who was asleep.

She saw a comic beside another patient's bed and borrowed it. She read, then – after a while – gave the comic back.

'Harry,' she shook his arm which was outside the covers. 'I don't want you to die.'

'Good,' sighed Harry.

'Oh,' said Abernetha, 'so you can hear me. What happened to you? I saw you in the cemetery with your new anorak on. It was you, wasn't it?'

Harry's eyes moved under his closed lids.

'Ooooh,' he sighed. 'What did you say, Abernetha?'

'I said, I saw you in the cemetery.'

'Why can't I move my head?'

'You've got a cage round it. The doctor says you've not to move your neck.'

'I'm in hospital?'

'Didn't you know?'

'I must've been out cold. That old woman.'

Harry opened his eyes. He found Abernetha and looked at her.

She said, 'What old woman? Surely they don't have old women on outdoor training courses?'

Abernetha saw Mum and Grandpa at the door to the ward, talking to a doctor. 'What about the old woman?'

'I think I remember falling,' whispered Harry, 'because the log was slippy with snow. She was waiting for me!' Harry's eyes opened wide. 'Abernetha!'

'Don't panic!' hissed Abernetha.

'But she was waiting! Abernetha—!'

'Be quiet, Harry! You mustn't move! I'm going to get Mum!'

Abernetha flitted from Harry's bedside and darted past beds to Mum and Grandpa.

'. . . prepare for the worst . . .' said the doctor.

'Mum,' said Abernetha, 'come and tell Harry to lie still. He's going on about an old woman. And he's wriggling like a worm . . . What? What have I said? Grandpa?'

But Grandpa, Mum and the doctor had rushed away and were shrieking quietly around Harry's bed.

When Abernetha joined them, Mum was crying and beaming, and Grandpa was frowning mightily and blinking, and even the doctor was glowing with relief.

'Has he moved too much?' asked Abernetha.

'He's all right!' wept Mum, and hugged Abernetha almost flat.

Grandpa's large hand patted Harry's arm.

The doctor smiled. 'He's out of danger. We'll get a little food into him, and you can come back this evening. You need some sleep,' he told Mum.

'Come on, Mary,' said Grandpa.

'Yes, come on, Mum,' said Abernetha, 'Stop fussing. I want my lunch.'

9

'When did you meet the woman again?' asked Abernetha, as Grandpa strode grinning into their tenement kitchen. 'Where's Mummy?'

'Bed,' grinned Grandpa. 'She sat with Harry all night at the hospital. I forced a sandwich down her before he woke up, so she isn't starving. Beans and pork sausage, wasn't it?'

Grandpa attacked the tin with the tin opener, and in a moment the beans and pork sausage were fizzing in a pan, and Grandpa put a Scotch pie in the microwave for himself.

'When did you sce her again?' asked Abernetha.

'Knives and forks,' ordered Grandpa, and Abernetha fumbled in the cutlery drawer. 'I saw her that same day,' said Grandpa. 'The day of the funeral. Old Miss Broom was buried at eleven in the morning. Then the woman gave me the fifty pounds not to fill in the grave—'

'I know all that, Grandpa.'

'Just reminding myself, Abernetha. Then Jennifer Antrim turned up—'

Abernetha sighed, and sat at her knife and fork while Grandpa stirred in the pan.

'The woman came back, running, after Jennifer left, and I was locking up the shed. She stopped, looking very stunned I might say, so that I was anxious for her. She stared towards the grave with its hump of earth; the grave seemed lonely with no headstone and no mourners, and just an old grave-digger . . .'

'Not so old,' said Abernetha, because that's what Grandpa wanted to hear.

'. . . and one beautiful lady—'

'Beautiful?'

'In my opinion, only. You may not have thought so, Abernetha, her not as young as your Mum—'

'I should hope not, since you fancied her, and Mum's your daughter.'

'The grave,' said Grandpa prodding a wooden spoon into the beans and pork sausage, 'looked lonely. Oh, wait, Abernetha,' said Grandpa as the microwave pinged that his pie was ready. 'Here! Here. Here. He-re,' gasped Grandpa serving the food to Abernetha and himself. 'Where was I?'

'The grave looked lonely. Good beans.'

'She really seemed dismayed that the grave was filled in; and I remembered the fifty pound note and held it out to her.

'She shook her head, and said, "Dig her up. Plcase. Please dig her up." She stepped close to me and gazed into my eyes. Her eyes were grey and solemn and beauti – and beautifully sad. "She's not dead," she cried softly.

'I shook my head.

'"Please!" she said.

'I said, "Nobody gets buried alive these days—"'

'Did they used to get buried alive?' asked Abernetha. 'I want some bread.' She went to the bread tin.

'Oh, yes,' said Grandpa.

'Do you want bread, Grandpa?'

'Thank you, Abernetha. Yes, please. I'll spread it for you. Sit in. Eat up. That's my good girl. Oh, yes, indeed. If you dig up an old graveyard, to build, say, a motorway across it—'

'Do people do that?'

'People can be very thoughtless, Abernetha. Now. Do you want to hear the story, or d'you want to hear about people being buried alive, or d'you want to hear about motorways?'

'Not motorways! But how did people get buried alive?'

'Because a hundred years ago, doctors couldn't be sure if a person was dead. But they thought they were sure – so people got buried alive. And as I was going to say, if you dig up an old graveyard, Abernetha, quite a few of the bodies aren't lying flat in their coffins, but all twisted about as if they'd been trying to escape.'

'Ooh.'

'Quite. I explained this to my lady – that it didn't happen nowadays – and that a doctor must have certified old Miss Broom as being dead; but she kept staring at me with those marvellous – with those grey eyes, until I wondered if maybe she was a bit mad. Which would've been a shame—'

'Because she was beautiful.'

'Mmm. Then I explained that an exhumation order—'

'What?'

'Exhumation. To exhume. To dig up, I suppose. An exhumation order was needed before I could open the grave, and policemen had to be there to see that everything was done properly . . .

'She lost her spirit then, that lady. She accepted her fifty pounds back. I thought she was going to faint, and I held her arms. Her whole weight sagged on to my hands; but your Grandpa's strong, and I kept her on her feet, and I put an arm round her while I unlocked the shed.

'I sat her on my chair in the shed, and lit the stove—'

'And,' said Abernetha, 'you made her a pot of tea. You always make tea for people, Grandpa. Can I have a biscuit?'

'Help yourself. But one only and clean your

teeth after. Yes, I made her a pot of tea. Do you want tea? I'm having some. Good pie, that.'

Grandpa rattled about until the teapot steamed on the table, and the biscuit tin began to get empty, because even Grandpa couldn't stop at just one biscuit, and Abernetha certainly didn't.

'She was dressed in a grey suit—'

'Your lady,' crunched Abernetha.

'The lady. As I said, not in mourning. Not in black, and she saw me looking, and she said, "I won't mourn for someone who's not dead. She's not! I've been to the police. I've been to the doctor who certified her! That's where I went after I spoke to you this morning! I thought if I hurried I could get her out before you filled in . . ."'

'She sipped her tea. She said, "It's too late, isn't it?"

'"Yes," I agreed.

'I said, "Why do you think she was alive? Is she a relative of yours?"'

'"Why do I think she's alive? Because I saw her. I saw her alive after the doctor told me she was dead!"'

10

'I could smell the earth off my clothes, Abernetha, as I sat in my shed with the woman. I can always smell earth after I've been digging. And I could smell the tea from our mugs, and a soapy freshness which was from her. I wondered if she was telling me a lie, when she said she had seen Miss Broom after the doctor had pronounced her dead; suspicious, I was, after listening to your Angry Agatha.

'But she wasn't telling me a lie.

'I waited for her to say more, but she sighed and drank the hot tea in great gulps, and when she raised her eyes to me, I saw tears in them; tears of hopelessness, because she knew I couldn't dig up her friend.

'"Was she a relative?" I asked again.

'"My aunt. Auntie Broom. Huh!" she laughed damply. "Auntie Broom. Dear Auntie Broom brought me up. We live in Warehouse Lane. It's very nice there. Our flat overlooks the river where the water rushes down the rocks looking like whisky . . ."

'She met my eye.

'I waited.

'"Auntie Broom," sighed the lady, "died in her sleep. Old people do. Her heart hadn't been strong, and climbing the stairs to our flat tired her. She had been more than tired that day – she was upset by Mrs Ramage who lives upstairs and, huh! ramages about all day. Auntie Broom always said that. Mrs Ramage ramaged about. We could hear her running above our heads to her front windows whenever someone went down the stairs. She had to see – you understand – who was going out. Or if either Auntie Broom or myself went into the back garden (which slopes down to the whisky river), Mrs Ramage would be at her back window, watching. She was just nosy, with nothing else to do. So we thought.

'"So we thought," whispered my lady,' said Grandpa, and sucked a biscuit.

'She said,' continued Grandpa, 'she said, "We thought she was just a nosy old woman – though not as old as Auntie Broom – with nothing better to do than ramage about. We did laugh. Not so's she could hear, you understand. We wouldn't be so rude. But Auntie could be mischievous at times, and that day – the day she went to bed and died – we went out, down the stairs, both of us, and we knew Mrs Ramage would be running to her front window to see who was going out, and Auntie grinned at me, and I said, what are you up to Auntie Broom? and she said, stay in the doorway, and out she went as if she was going to the shops, right out of sight. Then she came back, walking close under the windows where Mrs Ramage couldn't see her, and told me to go back up the stairs quietly, then down again noisily.

'"So I did. And I stopped in the doorway, and Auntie walked out of the doorway, again, as if she was going to the shops a second time! Then back she came, gurgling with laughter; then we both really left the doorway, and there was old Mrs Ramage leaning out her window, her fists on the sill, scowling horribly.

'"I hadn't noticed before, the size of her fists. Even looking up as high as her window, I could see how big her fists were. And how terrible her scowl was. Which made me anxious. Which was silly. It was only a joke. What could Mrs Ramage do? Why should she do anything? We didn't think she had a temper – but then, we didn't really know her.

'"When we came back from the shopping she was waiting for us on the stairs. Furious. She was furious. She said terrible things. Auntie Broom went quite pale. We said it was only a joke. We said we had every right to go in and out of the building as we pleased, that it wasn't our fault if she watched Auntie going out but failed to see her coming in.

'"But Mrs Ramage would have none of it. She said nobody made a fool of her. Nobody ever had and got away with it. Nobody in all her life had ever made a fool of her and got away with it, though some had tried.

'"She quite scared me, and Auntie Broom was shaking, so that I had to leave Mrs Ramage on the stairs and get Auntie up to our flat. I made her some sweet tea and put her to bed.

'"She lay very still and pale, though she was breathing.

'"I thought about Mrs Ramage being so angry, and – when we left her on the stair – being suddenly quiet, and as I looked back at her, oh! her eyes had glittered terribly in her fat face, glittering at Auntie! And I staggered, oh! as if her very glance had knocked me off-balance even though her glare was for Auntie. And I was very afraid.

'"I was afraid that Mrs Ramage was more than just a nosy fat old woman.

'"I was afraid that she might possess some dreadful wicked power!"

⁜

'"Oh, I know it sounds strange and absurd, but you didn't see that look in her eyes. You didn't feel the strength of that look, that glance, that deadly glare! So full of hurt and vengeance! And you didn't see poor Auntie Broom so pale and still in her bed!

'"Then she slept – Auntie slept. And I told myself not to be silly. I put our shopping into the kitchen cupboards. I put the meat and milk into the fridge. I peeped in at Auntie, so pale and still.

'"And cold. Her wrist was cold, and you know that this is the hottest summer in three hundred years! I phoned the doctor and he came immediately and told me that Auntie Broom was dead.

'"You can imagine the shock. And the fear. And the crazy thoughts about Mrs Ramage. Could her glance have killed dear Auntie Broom? What nonsense. What fantasy! What foolishness! Why, Auntie had a weak heart. She'd helped me carry the shopping, which she shouldn't have done. And she'd been upset at Mrs Ramage's anger, then she'd climbed the stairs to our flat, and her poor old heart had given out.

'"I sat with Auntie, watching her white, still face. I looked out at the whisky river foaming over the rocks – though not as wildly as usual, because of the lack of rain. Oh, and time passed, and I coped, somehow, and phoned people, and Auntie was taken away, then returned in her coffin to lie in our sitting-room so that friends could come and say goodbye.

'"Mrs Ramage came. She was so sorry. Sorry that Auntie was dead. Sorry about the quarrel. Sorry about everything, apparently, and I didn't believe her. I just didn't believe her, because in her eye was a sparkle of triumph as if she had cheated me in some way. As if she had got revenge.

'"Then last night – I can't believe we buried her this morning! Oh, last night, I dozed in a chair, exhausted, and wakened to find Auntie Broom standing beside me.

'"For a second, I thought I had dreamed that she was dead. Then I knew that she really was dead. But also, she was standing beside my chair. And her lips moved and her voice drifted as if from far away, saying that she wasn't – wasn't dead. Then she vanished, and I discovered it was late in the evening.

'"I had seen dear Auntie Broom, and I knew now she was alive, though her body was in its coffin in the sitting-room!

'"And I thought of her being buried before I could get anyone to listen to me, because I know how officials think: they think they know better than anyone else, especially a woman who tells a mad story about seeing her dead aunt.

'"And I panicked. I forgot that Auntie Broom was in the sitting-room. Maybe I could have wakened her. I could have tried! But I hurried through the evening streets thinking only of preventing Auntie from being buried, and that the best way to do that was to make sure the grave wasn't dug. But when I got here, to your graveyard, I saw that you had finished digging the grave.

'"So I filled it in. I wiped your spade and hung it on its nails behind your hut door . . . Luckily, you hadn't snapped the padlock properly shut, so I didn't need a key.

'"Then – after I got home – I wondered about what I had done. Was I really mad? I was certainly silly. How could I have seen Auntie Broom? I sweated with embarrassment at the thought of the grave-digger – you, dear man – finding the grave filled in.

'"Then I went to bed. And I felt better in the morning after some breakfast. Then I hoped that whoever had dug the grave had found time to dig it again in time for the funeral at eleven o'clock!

'"I calmed down.

'"One or two friends arrived in the flat, as company, and the undertakers came and put the lid on the coffin, shutting Auntie in. And I was feeling fairly bright, because sadness comes and goes when you can do nothing about what has happened. Well, I was feeling reasonably chirpy and sensible; in my bedroom; by myself; getting dressed for the funeral . . .

'"Oh.

'"Oh dear. I nearly fainted this time. I was dressed – in my black suit, black shoes – and I turned away from the mirror and Auntie was at my back.

'"I'm sure I shrieked. But not much, because my friends didn't hear in the other room.

'"And Auntie's mouth opened and I thought she told me not to let the undertakers take her away, because she wasn't dead. Then she vanished.

'"I sank onto my bed, and sat dazed.

'"Then I went into the sitting-room.

'"The undertakers were waiting for me to tell them to take Auntie away; but I couldn't. I stood near the coffin, listening. I touched the lid, wanting to knock to see if she would reply, because, I knew, of course, that I hadn't seen Auntie in her body, in my bedroom, but her ghost. I wanted to knock and ask if she was awake, but I couldn't, not with the undertakers there.

'"Then the undertakers kindly left me alone. They just went very quietly. How understanding. I knocked on the coffin. I whispered Auntie's name. I knocked loudly. I shook the coffin until poor Auntie's body must have been jiggled very improperly.

'"Then I went back to my bedroom and told myself not to be silly, and Auntie appeared again. Close beside me, staring into my eyes, pleading, and her mouth moved and her words reached me as if from a vast distance, saying that she wasn't dead, but trapped by the Power of Darkness."'

11

'"I didn't know what the Power of Darkness was, and I didn't think about it. I rushed through to the undertakers and told them that Auntie wasn't dead, and they assured me that she was, that they had a copy of the death certificate. But I went on so fiercely that they opened the coffin, and showed me Auntie so still and white, not breathing, and not even really white because the undertaker had put make-up on her so that she looked not too bad for the people who had come to say goodbye. She certainly looked dead. I couldn't blame the undertakers for calming me, then shutting the coffin, and taking it downstairs to the street and into the hearse.

'"I changed out of my black suit and put on my grey suit and grey shoes because part of me believed that Auntie wasn't dead, therefore I wasn't going to mourn her by wearing black.

'"I told myself for the hundredth time not to be silly; that I was shocked at Auntie dying so suddenly, and I was just imagining she had come back.

'"I went down the stairs with my friends. Mrs Ramage followed us from her flat and smiled from the doorway as we drove off heading for the cemetery.

'"Looking over Mrs Ramage's shoulder, I saw Auntie Broom, her mouth moving, her voice still reaching me, saying that she wasn't dead, and don't let them bury me!"'

Grandpa made a smile for Abernetha.

'Is she bonkers, Grandpa? Your lady?'

'Rachel,' said Grandpa. 'Her name is Rachel.

And I did wonder if she was bonkers. But what was I to do if she wasn't? As I told her, I couldn't dig up old Miss Broom. But she held my hand—'

'Oh, Grandpa!' smiled Abernetha.

'—as we sat in my shed, and she wept, then she insisted on washing our tea mugs. I know how she felt,' said Grandpa solemnly, and Abernetha thought of Harry being almost dead in hospital, so that she too, knew how Rachel had felt.

Abernetha sat dabbing biscuit crumbs off her plate.

Grandpa's story floated in her mind.

Abernetha was pleased that Grandpa fancied the lady, Rachel, and that Rachel (Abernetha thought) fancied Grandpa.

'What's the Power of Darkness?' asked Abernetha.

'Cigar,' said Grandpa, rising suddenly, and gathering dishes from the table.

By the time Abernetha had held a cigar to

a hot coal and burnt perhaps quarter of the cigar away, Grandpa had cleared and wiped the table. He took the cigar and looked at it suspiciously. He sat in his chair, smoking.

He said, 'D'you want to go and see her? Rachel? I told her about you.'

'All right. What's the Power of Darkness?'

'I'll phone her,' said Grandpa, and leapt up like a much younger man.

Abernetha heard him murmuring and laughing into the phone in the hall.

Then she heard him open the door to Mum's room. She heard the door shut, and Grandpa came back and sank into his chair.

'Your Mum's smiling in her sleep. We'll go when I finish my cigar. What did you ask me, Abernetha?'

Abernetha gave Grandpa a look.

'Oh, yes,' he said hurriedly, 'the Power of Darkness.'

But he frowned, then smoke escaped from

his lips in a stream that attacked the clock on the mantelpiece. Grandpa shook his head. 'It's a terrible thing, the Power of Darkness. Most people suffer from it Abernetha, though they don't realise. They feed it to themselves with black thoughts; thoughts as black as the shadows in the cemetery; thoughts that are really fears or hatred, so that they fill their minds with fear or hatred and the world becomes fearful or hateful . . .

'Does that make sense? Yes! Yes! Of course, it does. But some people, Abernetha, become so filled with hate, that it spills out of them, and people – without knowing quite why – stay out of their way—'

'Angry Agatha,' murmured Abernetha.

'Right,' said Grandpa, sounding surprised. 'I didn't think of her. Poor Jennifer Antrim. She has gathered the Power of Darkness very early in life. But I was thinking of Mrs Ramage. She's old, you know, and has been gathering hate all her life perhaps, so that it really does spill out. Oh, I've seen it a few times, Abernetha! Don't smile at it!

'And my Rachel saw it in Mrs Ramage the day Miss Broom died. Though Rachel didn't realise at the time. Remember, Abernetha, the glare that Rachel thought almost knocked her over? That was the Power of Darkness spilling out of Mrs Ramage, though why that woman should be full of hate, I can't tell, but she did say that nobody made a fool of her and got away with it.'

Grandpa scowled and smoked. He said, 'That's what the Power of Darkness is.'

Abernetha tried to bend the flames in the fireplace by glaring at them, but they danced on quite happily.

'Hmn,' said Grandpa, and got up. He scowled as he prepared a stew, making sure his cigar ash fell on the floor instead of into the meat.

He scraped carrots and chopped onions as

if he wanted to hurt them. He flung them into the pot after the meat. He stuck the hot end of his cigar into the unlit gas beneath the pot until the gas said, 'Bloomph!' and burned. He caught Abernetha's eye.

'We should go to see Rachel,' he growled.

He set the timer on the cooker. 'Half-past three now. This should cook safely for half-an-hour. The pinger will wake your mum, and she can add some water until the stew's cooked through. She'll be hungry.'

He glanced towards the window. 'It's dark already. Is it still snowing? Take a look, Abernetha, while I fetch my wellingtons. Do your teeth, after these biscuits. Get wrapped up. I'll leave a note for your mum. Let's go! Let's go!'

‡

'This is it,' said Grandpa, clutching Abernetha's hand, looking up into the dark dropping snow at the building which towered above the glow of the street lights. Most windows in the building were lit. And the snow sped down into Abernetha's eyes. 'Used to be a warehouse,' said Grandpa. 'Warehouse Lane, you know.'

'I remember.'

'Press the buzzer on the door. The one that says BROOM. RAMAGE is above it, see?'

The door spoke, though Abernetha couldn't make out the words squeezing from the metal speaker.

Grandpa said, 'It's us.' And the door opened, and in they went, stomping to shake snow from their clothes.

'Come up!' called a lady's voice, and they climbed the stairs.

They bustled into the warmth of Rachel's flat.

Rachel hesitated, then kissed Grandpa on the mouth, then smiled at Abernetha.

Abernetha stared. She had never seen anyone kiss Grandpa on the mouth. Mum kissed him on the cheek. Abernetha kissed his cheek or his nose.

'Abernetha,' warned Grandpa, and Abernetha remembered she was staring, and said, 'Hello,' because she liked Rachel with her black hair and white smile. Though the smile seemed weary to Abernetha.

They sat in Rachel's sitting-room, and refused tea. Then Grandpa accepted a glass of something, and Abernetha sipped orange juice.

Rachel smiled at Abernetha, but mainly she smiled at Grandpa, and Grandpa raised one eyebrow, as if not believing he was with Rachel.

'Did you see her?' asked Rachel. 'Mrs Ramage? When you pressed the buzzer?'

'No,' said Grandpa.

'I heard her running to the front window.'

'The snow got into my eyes,' said Abernetha, thinking of fat Mrs Ramage thudding across her floor in the flat upstairs.

'She keeps meeting me,' said Rachel, 'on the

stairs. In the street. She does it deliberately. She does. I'm sure. And that look. I told you, Arthur, that look of triumph—'

Abernetha was surprised at hearing Rachel use Grandpa's name. Then she wasn't surprised. What else would she call him?

'—that look of triumph, as if she has cheated me somehow. As if she has got her revenge for our girlish joke.' She turned to Abernetha. 'My aunt went out of the building then came back so that Mrs Ramage couldn't see her, then went out again—'

'Grandpa told me,' said Abernetha.

'Oh. I must sound very foolish. And nervous.'

'You don't talk the way Grandpa said,' said Abernetha.

'I'm a bit frightened,' admitted Rachel. 'Have you seen her fists? No. How could you—!'

Rachel's voice rose to a squeak as a doorbell rang. The door to the flat, thought

Abernetha, not the buzzer on the door to the street.

'It's her,' whispered Rachel, and she stood up. 'She heard you coming here, and wants to know who you are. She keeps asking about you! She wants to know everything!'

12

'I'll answer the door,' offered Grandpa, putting down his drink, and standing up.

'No, I can deal with her.' Rachel walked out of the sitting-room.

Abernetha heard Rachel's voice, nervous, but firm. 'Mrs Ramage. I don't use sugar, so I can't lend you any. Yes, I expect it is why I am slim. Yes, you may have heard visitors. You can't join us for tea, Mrs Ramage, because we're not drinking tea—'

Abernetha heard Rachel gasp. Then feet shook the floor and Mrs Ramage stomped into the sitting-room. Rachel hesitated behind her, her face angry.

Mrs Ramage smiled at Grandpa then grinned down on Abernetha. Abernetha didn't like the way the woman had barged in, and she didn't like her grin because Mrs Ramage's eyes were like crow's eyes, hard and ready to hate.

Rachel's grey eyes were also ready to hate, for they blazed behind Mrs Ramage's back, and her foot tapped with fury on the carpet.

Rachel gasped, 'Now you've seen what you want, perhaps you would leave!'

'I'm Mrs Ramage,' said Mrs Ramage turning to Grandpa who was much taller. 'I live upstairs.' Her face pointed at the ceiling, but her eyes stayed on Grandpa.

Grandpa said, 'Are you,' and shut his mouth.

Abernetha was startled at Grandpa not introducing himself. She had never heard him being rude before.

Mrs Ramage bent to Abernetha, and her cheeks changed shape as fat dragged them downwards, and her smile tightened nastily as she said, 'And what's your name, little girl?'

'Her name is her own,' said Grandpa, and Mrs Ramage's crow eyes glittered on Abernetha; then she turned from Abernetha who said nothing, and looked at Grandpa.

Abernetha noticed Mrs Ramage's fists curl into large balls, and wondered if she was going to hit Grandpa; and maybe Mrs Ramage wanted to, for her smile stretched into a grimace of rage; and Grandpa tilted his head and said nothing; waiting. Then Mrs Ramage whirled away from him, and the floor shook as she thudded past Rachel and banged from the flat.

Grandpa breathed out long and slow.

Rachel stood beside him, and rested her brow on his shoulder.

Grandpa's hand appeared around Rachel's head and patted her hair.

Abernetha told herself not to be surprised at Grandpa patting Rachel.

She was just surprised that he knew Rachel well enough.

Rachel saw Abernetha watching, and smiled palely. She said, 'Your Grandpa's good to me. Do you mind?'

'I don't mind.'

'I'm sorry about Mrs Ramage bursting in. I can't believe she did it. In she burst—'

'Sit down,' said Grandpa, and Rachel sat and sipped her drink.

Grandpa chatted to Rachel, until she smiled properly.

Abernetha wandered around the room. She gazed at a photograph of Rachel with an old lady; Miss Broom, guessed Abernetha.

Abernetha peered out of the back window, but only her reflection peered in from the darkness, and snowflakes thudded silently onto the glass. Abernetha imagined she could hear the whisky river rushing over the rocks beyond the garden. But she could see nothing outside.

She said, 'We're visiting Harry tonight.'

And Grandpa said, 'We'd better go. Will you be all right, Rachel?'

'Is this Auntie Broom?' asked Abernetha, lifting the photograph. 'She's got lovely frothy white hair.'

'Yes, it is.' Rachel rose and held out her hand for the photograph. She showed it to Grandpa, and he nodded over it as if he'd seen it before, then he stopped nodding, and simply looked.

Then he put his thumb over Miss Broom's hair, and Abernetha – pushing close to Grandpa – saw just the old lady's face.

'What?' asked Rachel.

'I saw her,' said Grandpa, letting Rachel take the photograph. 'The day I dug her grave. You remember the story, Abernetha? Behind the white stone cross—'

'The face among the leaves,' said Abernetha.

'The face among the leaves,' agreed Grandpa, 'where there weren't any leaves. And I may be wrong, because it was during the summer which was months ago, but I'm pretty sure that the face I saw, was the face in your photograph, Rachel – the face of your dear Auntie Broom.'

⁂

Abernetha walked between Grandpa and Mum, along the hospital corridor.

Mum said, 'Rachel was upset?'

'She was,' replied Grandpa. 'But I had to leave her, to see that you were all right, Mary, and that the stew wasn't burned.'

They marched into the ward, and found Harry smiling from his cage.

'Hey, Mum. Grandpa. Hello, monster.' Harry bent his eyes round at Abernetha; and grapes appeared and Lucozade; and How are you feeling, Harry? Hello, nurse, is he really getting better? That's wonderful! But what happened? You said you fell off a log?

'Why were you on a log?' demanded Abernetha. 'And what old woman did you mean? Were you delirious?'

'An old woman?' smiled Mum. 'I don't think so. No old women trying to cross a river on just a log for a bridge.'

'There really was an old woman, Mum,' said Harry, 'though she wasn't on the log. I don't know where she popped up from. The log was slippy, but the next thing I knew I was some distance from the river and she was waiting—'

'You mean she appeared out of nowhere?' sighed Abernetha, pretending she didn't believe Harry; but she did believe him, because so many strange things had been happening.

'I don't believe it either, Abernetha,' said Harry, 'but that's what I saw. An old woman with white hair sticking up like candy floss—'

Abernetha remembered the photograph of Miss Broom: she had hair which looked like white candy floss.

'You must've been dreaming,' said Abernetha doubtfully.

'No.'

'No?'

'No. I've told myself I was dreaming; but I know I wasn't. Grandpa,' said Harry.

Grandpa patted Harry's shoulder.

'Mum?' said Harry.

Mum held Harry's hand.

'It's really, really weird, Mum.'

'Have you had something to eat?' asked Mum.

'Yes. I want to tell you about what happened—'

'Pour Harry some Lucozade, Dad,' said Mum.

'I can't drink it,' protested Harry. 'I need a straw. Mum!' he cried as Mum turned to find a nurse. 'Mum! I don't want a drink! I want you to listen!'

'I'm sorry, Harry,' sniffed Mum. 'I just thought—'

Harry closed his eyes.

'Mary,' warned Grandpa quietly, 'don't tire him. Let him tell us.'

So Mum sat, stiff as cardboard, until Harry opened his eyes to see if it was safe to come out.

'I don't actually remember falling into the river. When the old woman startled me, I found I was among the trees not too far from the log – the bridge. You'd have loved the snow, Abernetha. Knee-deep it was. And the sky full of clouds ready to drop more—'

'You were among the trees?' asked Grandpa.

'Yes, Grandpa. I can't explain it. But I was

suddenly among the trees, and the rest of the team were on the river bank, and Ron – he's the leader – was giving orders, and sounding really, really worried. I've been thinking about it, Grandpa – Mum . . . I think they were fishing me out of the water.'

Mum put a hand to her mouth.

'I was going to join them, you know. Help, you know. I'd only been on the course a few hours, but I reckoned I was stronger than anybody else, and if somebody needed rescuing . . . I didn't think, then, that it was me . . .

'Then I found myself beside the old woman. Weird, she was, Abernetha, with all her froth of hair—'

Abernetha nodded. 'That's right!' she whispered, and Harry blinked at her, but continued.

'– and no anorak. No boots, I don't think. I can't really say I saw her feet, but I had the impression she had no boots. She was wearing a black dress—'

'Weren't you cold?' asked Abernetha.

'No. And neither was the old woman. She saw me looking at her clothes and just shook her head as if it didn't matter; and she took my hand and tried to drag me away through the trees; and I said something about helping the others, but she said she needed me. She had come to me specially because I was the grave-digger's grandson and she had waited months for a chance to meet me. And, gosh, Grandpa, I thought then, for a second, that I was dreaming.

'Her words were a dream-sort-of-thing to say! That I was the grave-digger's grandson! And waiting until I fell into the river until she met me! That, and not being cold, and her not being cold. And, anyway, Abernetha, I went through the trees with her, thinking somebody she was with had hurt themselves, but I was confused, because though I could see her as well as I can see you . . . I mean, Mum, an old lady out in deep snow wearing a black dress without a damp mark round the hem . . . Creepy isn't the word—'

'And it was real?' demanded Abernetha.

'Oh, it was real, all right. Grandpa, I was getting scared.'

'Get on with the story!' said Abernetha.

'Yes. Where was I? Right. She led me through the trees, and *that* was weird! because it was no effort! You know what it's like walking through deep snow! You've gotta lift your knees up to your chest almost, and keep your balance, but, Grandpa . . . Mum . . . we flitted through the forest—'

'Forest?' said Abernetha.

'Oh, yes. Miles from anywhere. I couldn't imagine where we were going. But I followed her, the old lady pulling my hand, really, really shifting through the snow. I mean, nobody could walk at that speed! But we both were shifting, really! without any effort.'

Harry closed his eyes inside his head cage.

'You all right, Harry?' asked Grandpa.

'Yes.'

'We'll let you sleep now. You can tell us the rest later.'

Abernetha felt indignant. 'Grandpa! He can't sleep now! He's just started a story!'

'Later,' said Grandpa firmly. 'Mary?' And Mum nodded and tried to kiss Harry through his cage, but couldn't, and kissed his hand.

'See you in the morning,' whispered Mum.

'Mm,' said Harry, his eyes still closed.

'See you later!' grumped Abernetha, and Harry smiled, then sighed into sleep.

13

Monday morning; Abernetha woke to the phone ringing, and Mum's voice, 'Oh, yes. Yes. I'm sure Abernetha will. She likes the snow. What about tomorrow? You'll phone again. Thank you. Goodbye. Abernetha!' called Mum. 'Breakfast!'

Abernetha headed for her breakfast in the kitchen, kissed Grandpa's cheek, then frowned up at her mother.

'Oh,' said Mum, understanding that Abernetha's frown was a question. 'That was the school on the phone. You don't have to go in today. Too much snow – '

'Hey!' grinned Abernetha.

'– but they asked if you would tell the other children in the street – '

'Oh, Mum!'

'– and I said you would. There are only two or three – '

'Oh, Mu-um! Angry Agatha's one of them! I can't go and see her!'

'Of course you can. Now eat a bit of toast and just do it! Before they leave for school.'

'Oh, Mum.' But Abernetha stuck marmalady toast in her mouth and hauled on her wellingtons. She munched into her anorak. She went out the front door of the flat onto the snowy pavement, rang two doorbells to give them the good news that school was shut, then headed towards Angry Agatha's flat.

Abernetha groaned but pressed the doorbell.

The door jumped open and Jennifer Antrim stared from her thin little face at Abernetha.

Abernetha drew in a breath to speak, but Jennifer's mouth bit in, with: 'Your brother's in hospital! He's going to die! And your grandfather stole fifty pounds last summer and I reported him to the town hall so he'll lose his job—'

Abernetha felt her face crinkle in contempt. What a load of rubbish. But she didn't say it was a load of rubbish, she said: 'You're a skinny little wart, Angry Agatha! And I hope your head falls off! I hope your eyes jump out and a dog eats them! I hope—'

Abernetha stopped talking and stepped back as Jennifer's mother surged up behind her. 'Did you come here to make trouble?'

'She started it,' said Abernetha.

'Get your schoolbag!' Mrs Antrim hauled Jennifer back and bent her down, then hauled her straight, a schoolbag now in Jennifer's grasp. 'Put this on!' ordered Mrs Antrim and her arm vanished behind the open door and reappeared holding an anorak in a fist almost as big as Mrs Ramage's. She pushed the anorak against Jennifer's chest. 'Now get to school! And don't you come here making trouble!' she shouted at Abernetha; and she pushed Jennifer outside into the snow and slammed the door.

Abernetha gaped. She had never seen anyone treated so cruelly.

Jennifer dropped her schoolbag and slouched into her anorak.

Her thin little face scowled, though whether with concentrating on zipping her anorak, or to keep from crying, Abernetha wasn't sure.

Abernetha said, 'Does your Mum treat you like that all the time?'

'Like what? What's it to you? I don't want you with me going to school! Your grandfather steals money and spits on coffins—'

'Oh, shut up. I wouldn't go to school with you if you were the last . . .'

Abernetha couldn't think how to finish what she was saying. Her heart wasn't really in hurting Angry Agatha after seeing how her mum had flung her out.

'What?' said Jennifer, seeing Abernetha's face.

'School's shut,' said Abernetha. 'That's what I came to tell you. Why are you so rude?'

'I'm not rude! You're rude! I've seen you in class with your knickers showing—!'

'Oh,' said Abernetha, and walked away.

Jennifer Antrim was a poor little thing.

Like a tarantula's a poor little thing, thought Abernetha.

Or a rock with bugs under it.

Or—

'Where are you going?'

Abernetha turned.

'Home, of course.' Abernetha wondered why Jennifer didn't ring her doorbell and tell her mother there was no school.

'Maybe,' said Jennifer, 'your grandfather's not that bad.'

Abernetha shrugged.

'Maybe he didn't spit on a coffin.'

'Why don't you go back in?' asked Abernetha, nodding at Jennifer Antrim's front door.

'Don't want to.'

'Well, I've got to go home. I haven't had my breakfast.' And she walked away, the snow kicking from her wellingtons, cars throwing up a wall of white spray from the road.

A snowball landed beside Abernetha, but she wasn't interested in Angry Agatha. She was interested in hearing the rest of Harry's weird story. Being off school meant she could visit him, maybe this morning.

Mum let her in, and Abernetha waggled out of her wellies, and helped herself to breakfast in the kitchen. 'I'm off to work,' smiled Mum. 'Dad, will you look after Abernetha? You don't have any digging to do? And you'll find time to go to the hospital? Tell them I'll phone—'

'I'll keep her with me,' Grandpa assured her; and Mum left.

Grandpa was reaching for a cigar, and Abernetha was eating Rice Krispies, when the front door bell rang.

'Postman,' said Grandpa. 'I'll get it.'

But it wasn't the postman.

It was Angry Agatha – poor little thing.

14

Of course, when Grandpa opened the door, Abernetha didn't *know* it was Angry Agatha.

She only heard Grandpa, say, 'Yes?' and she knew it wasn't the postman.

Then Grandpa said, 'I don't want to stand here with the door open.'

Silence.

'Do you want something?'

More silence.

'Perhaps,' Grandpa sighed loudly enough for Abernetha in the kitchen to hear, 'you'd better come in until you find your tongue.'

And Abernetha stared towards the hall over her spoonful of Rice Krispies.

She frowned when Angry Agatha stepped in. She shoved her Krispies into her mouth, and went on frowning as Grandpa allowed the thin angry child into the kitchen.

Angry Agatha stared at the fire which welcomed her with heat. She dropped her schoolbag and knelt before the flames.

'Would you like some breakfast?' asked Grandpa.

Angry Agatha turned from the fire and looked at the table with its cereal packets, and butter and toast and marmalade and Grandpa's dirty plate with bacon rind on it and a scrape of egg yolk. She stood up. 'Some of that,' she said, nodding at Grandpa's plate.

'You've got a cheek,' said Abernetha. 'Doesn't your mother feed you?'

'No,' said Jennifer Antrim, still gazing at the plate.

Abernetha looked at Grandpa. He raised his eyebrows, and turned to the cooker. He laid bacon in the frying pan then cracked in an egg.

Jennifer walked over to the cooker and watched. She looked up at Grandpa. She said, 'Are you doing that for me?'

'You said you wanted it—'

'I'm not giving you anything!'

'No. No, I suppose not.'

'Then why are you doing it? Why did you let me in? You've kidnapped me! I'm going to tell the police!' She glanced at the clock on the mantelpiece. 'You brought me into your house at eighteen minutes past eight and forced me to eat your breakfast—'

Grandpa gazed coolly down on the child.

Jennifer Antrim backed away until she was in a far corner of the kitchen. She slid down, and sat on the floor. 'I'm going to tell the police!' she muttered.

Grandpa turned the bacon over.

Jennifer raised her face, so that her nose sniffed the bacon smell.

'Ready in a minute,' said Grandpa. 'So if you're going for the police you'd better go now, because the bacon will be burnt before you're back.'

He held a plate over the frying pan to warm it.

Then he served the bacon and egg on the warm plate and put it on the table. He cleared away his dirty plate and Mum's dirty plates, and the cups, and began washing them.

Abernetha finished her cereal. She wondered if Jennifer Antrim was mad. She certainly behaved very strangely.

But then, so did her mother, pushing her out of the house like that.

'Aren't you going to eat it?' asked Abernetha curiously.

Jennifer crept out of the corner and stood

up. She walked to the table and looked at the food. She looked at Grandpa, but he was busy with the dishes.

She slid onto the chair and gobbled, using her knife and fork clumsily.

'D'you want some toast?' asked Abernetha, pushing the toast rack to her. 'It's still warm – you don't have to pay for it!' she groaned, as Jennifer hesitated.

The thin child snatched the toast, biting it without butter.

'What did you mean,' asked Abernetha, 'that your mother doesn't feed you? You must eat something.'

'I feed myself,' mumbled Jennifer through her chewing.

'Doesn't she make your tea at night?'

'I make it for myself.'

'Who makes your Mum's tea?'

'She does. What's wrong with that? She makes her tea and my dad makes his, and

I make mine. Then we eat our own. That's fair, isn't it?'

'It isn't very nice,' commented Abernetha. 'Why did you come to our door?'

Jennifer wiped her toast around her eggy plate. She shrugged.

'You could have gone home,' said Abernetha.

'She told me to go to school.'

'But—'

'I have to do what she tells me.'

'But you didn't go to school.'

'I had to pretend.' Jennifer stared at her empty plate. She stared at the marmalade.

'Take another bit of toast,' said Abernetha. Then she went to lean on Grandpa as he dried the dishes so that she didn't have to look at Jennifer's thin sad face. She heard Jennifer's knife spreading the toast. She heard Jennifer's teeth biting the toast.

She heard Jennifer's body sobbing.

Abernetha and Grandpa went and sat at the kitchen table.

Jennifer sobbed, a bite of toast trapped in her cheek.

Abernetha sighed, 'Poor little thing,' quietly.

Then Jennifer stopped sobbing, and sat, toast still in her cheek, gazing at the tablecloth, tears dripping from her lashes.

'How did you know Miss Broom's name?' asked Abernetha.

'Who?' whispered Jennifer.

'The old lady in the coffin. Last summer. You were up a tree.'

'Oh, her. My Gran lives upstairs from her. My Gran's Mrs Ramage, and nobody gets away with anything in *her* house.' And Angry Agatha gulped her toast then howled like any other little girl who felt that no one in the whole world loved her.

15

There is nothing like hot chocolate to take away tears; so in a minute, Grandpa had milk warming and was stirring in the chocolate; and in another minute the chocolatey smell filled the kitchen, and in another minute, a mug of chocolate was on the table under Jennifer Antrim's nose.

It was a long time, though, before she sipped it; and by then she had used most of a box of tissues that Abernetha had brought from Mum's bedroom.

'Isn't your Gran nice to you?' asked Abernetha eventually, thinking how terrible

Mrs Ramage had looked in Rachel's flat the day before.

'Of course she is! Everything's fair in Gran's house, too! If I drop something, she slaps me. That's fair, isn't it?'

'Fair?' whispered Abernetha.

'If I make a noise she hits me with her fist. It's only fair. And if I dodge away, she tells my Mum and *she* hits me. Things have to be fair. You don't cross my Gran. The girl in the newsagent's wasn't polite to Gran last week. And do you know what Gran did? Ha! Ha! She bought a coke and spilled it over all the newspapers! Huh! Huh! Huh! That was fair, wasn't it? Wasn't it?' repeated Jennifer, as Abernetha and Grandpa stared at her in dismay.

'Well, it was!' cried the child's thin sad face.

'Fair!' whispered Abernetha again.

'And what does she do,' asked Grandpa,

'if someone... let me see... plays a joke on her?'

Jennifer gulped her chocolate, her eyes still wet, but laughing. 'Well, that Miss Broom played a joke, and Gran got her own back! It's not right playing jokes on an old woman who lives alone and has no company except a sour child! Gran calls it "turning the enemy to stone" like in fairy tales, though it isn't really that! It's better! Better! Great revenge! She gives her enemy a look, does Gran! Wham! and the life goes out of them! Huh! Huh! Huh! Not dead though! Oh, no, not dead! That would be wicked, says my Gran. Just knocks the life out of them to make things fair! It's not Gran's fault if doctors don't know the difference and say they're dead and get them put into their coffins and buried! It's you that killed her!' she shrieked at Grandpa. 'You put her in the ground! You covered her with earth and put in the gravestone telling everybody she was dead! My Gran didn't do it! My Gran didn't do anything except make things fair! Life's got to be fair or it's not worth anything!'

Jennifer Antrim sat gasping, staring wildly.

Abernetha saw that Grandpa's face was white.

He said, 'She was alive?'

'Of course,' shuddered Jennifer.

'Grandpa,' said Abernetha. 'What does it mean?'

'She was alive!' whispered Grandpa. 'I didn't listen to Rachel at the time, and I filled in the grave. She was alive.'

'She couldn't have been!' cried Abernetha, though she too, feared that Miss Broom had been alive. She turned on Jennifer Antrim. 'Why did you come here you little beast? Just to tell us your horrible lies? Well, how would you like us to bury *you*? My Grandpa can dig a grave in five minutes and drop you in it and cover you up then see if you think it's fair—!'

'Abernetha!' thundered Grandpa.

But he was too late, because horror showed in Jennifer Antrim's face, and she fled, rushing from the kitchen, into the hall. Then the front door crashed open against the wall and cold air swarmed into the kitchen to find out what all the shouting was about.

⁜

Abernetha swung her legs on a chair in a waiting-room in the town hall.

Grandpa had gone off to talk to someone beyond a door with *Mr B Jeffries* painted on the glass.

Grandpa had been behind the door for a long time, and Abernetha had heard his voice raised, and Mr B Jeffries' voice answering soothingly.

Then Grandpa came backwards out the door and Mr B Jeffries' hand shook Grandpa's hand, and Mr B Jeffries' voice said, 'No worrying now. You've done the right thing all along the line.'

Then the door shut, and Abernetha followed Grandpa out into the snow.

'He said they can't dig her up on the say-so of a demented child. And he's right, of course, Abernetha. Your Angry Agatha is a liar and a trouble-maker—'

'Rachel isn't.'

'No. No, Rachel isn't,' agreed Grandpa. 'According to Mr Jeffries, Rachel was probably upset at her aunt's sudden death and just imagined that the old lady had reappeared. And he's probably right. He was very nice, considering how nutty I must have sounded.'

'Are we going to the hospital to see Harry?'

'I rather think,' said Grandpa, 'we're going to see Mrs Ramage.'

16

Abernetha held Grandpa's hand as they trudged through the city. The sky stood clear and bright overhead and Abernetha wondered if it was lunch time. Snow was piled in the gutters for Abernetha to jump on.

Grandpa popped into a shop that sold electronic equipment and reappeared before Abernetha's feet had time to get cold.

When Abernetha and Grandpa reached Warehouse Lane, Grandpa did not press the buzzer beside the name BROOM; he pressed the buzzer beside the name RAMAGE.

'Yes?' said the metal speaker on the door, sounding puzzled.

'Mrs Ramage?' said Grandpa, and his voice shook ever so slightly.

'Who's there?'

'I met you yesterday in Miss Broom's flat. I want to talk to you.'

The metal box said nothing.

Abernetha wished Grandpa had taken her to see Harry.

The door clicked, and Grandpa pushed it open.

Abernetha followed him up the stairs. She said, 'What about Rachel?'

'I don't want her involved,' said Grandpa; so they passed Rachel's door, and climbed to the floor above.

The door to Mrs Ramage's flat opened, and the old woman stared at them, her eyes like black lights.

Mrs Ramage stood aside without speaking, and Grandpa led Abernetha inside.

Mrs Ramage took them into a room which overlooked the whisky river. Abernetha was disappointed that the room was like anybody's sitting-room. No wicked pictures hung on the walls, and the only smell was coffee.

'Sit,' ordered Mrs Ramage, and Grandpa sat, then Abernetha sat in a chair near him.

'The little girl with no name,' said Mrs Ramage, her eyes shining darkly at Abernetha. 'And the man with no name.' She glared at Grandpa. 'Maybe you've come to apologise for not introducing yourself, if so – forget it. I don't accept apologies. You do wrong to me – I do wrong to you. That's fair.'

'Like you did to Miss Broom,' said Grandpa a little breathlessly.

And, oh, a slow smile bulged the woman's cheeks into pink balloons, until her eyes were black slits; then she turned her back and laughed out loud towards the whisky river, fat shaking on her bones.

'Well!' cried Mrs Ramage heartily, turning, beaming on Abernetha and Grandpa. 'Aren't you going to introduce yourselves? You come barging in here—'

'No,' said Grandpa.

'You invited us in,' said Abernetha indignantly.

'– after insulting me yesterday—'

'We never!' cried Abernetha.

Mrs Ramage bent suddenly, her huge face almost touching Abernetha's. 'You didn't introduce yourselves! That's an insult! As if you didn't trust me with your names!'

'Ah!' said Grandpa, and stood up.

Mrs Ramage whirled at him, then stopped, for Grandpa was a head taller than Mrs Ramage, though she was broader with fat; and her fists gathered into balls at her side, and they were quite as big as Grandpa's fists. Not that Grandpa would ever hit Mrs Ramage.

Grandpa would never hit anyone.

'What did you do,' said Grandpa into Mrs Ramage's glaring face, 'to old Miss Broom?'

A sly look slid across Mrs Ramage's eyes. She turned from Grandpa, and sat down in an armchair.

'Do?' she trilled.

Grandpa waited.

'Why should I have done something to Miss Broom? If she wants to make a fool of me that's her look out. If she thinks she can play silly tricks on me she knows better now, doesn't she? Going out of the front door then sneaking back, and going out again, amusing herself at my expense! Nobody makes a fool of Maisie Ramage!

'I'll tell you what I did! I took away her life! How do you like that? man with no name! How do you like that? little girl with no name! D'you think I don't know who you are? You're the grave-digger. And you, little girl, you are the grave-digger's granddaughter – Abernetha.

Oh, I know your name, and knowing your name means that I can use it against you; I can hug it to me in my head, and pile my thoughts around it until my thoughts pile around you and knock you over, or take the life out of you, like I took it out of that old Broom woman, so that everyone thinks she is dead . . .'

Abernetha frowned at Mrs Ramage, wondering if she was as mad as Angry Agatha.

'. . . but she wasn't dead. Dead enough – only – to silence her heart and chill her bones, but not enough to kill her. Not dead-as-a-doornail dead. Not shot-through-the-head dead. Not run-over-by-a-bus dead! Just dead enough to get herself put into her grave and left.

'But alive enough, Mr Grave-digger, to *know!*'

Mrs Ramage sat in her armchair, panting after her outburst; and grinning at Grandpa as if she knew she had hurt him.

But Grandpa didn't seem hurt, to Abernetha.

And Mrs Ramage saw that he wasn't hurt, and she stopped grinning, and frowned.

'Thank you,' murmured Grandpa. And stood up. 'Abernetha.'

Abernetha stood up.

'Is that all?' scowled Mrs Ramage. She struggled out of her chair and glared.

'Yes, thank you.'

'What are you up to?'

'Thank you.' Grandpa took Abernetha to the door.

'Stop thanking me!' thundered Mrs Ramage.

Grandpa opened the door onto the stairs and pushed Abernetha ahead of him. He smiled at Mrs Ramage.

'Thank you,' he chirruped, and ran down the stairs with his hand on Abernetha's shoulder.

'Shouldn't we see Rachel now?' asked Abernetha as they descended past Rachel's door.

'What are you up to!' bellowed Mrs Ramage from up the stairs.

'We're going back to the town hall,' said Grandpa to Abernetha. 'And Rachel's at work, anyway. Open the street door, Abernetha. Into the fresh air. What a monstrous old woman.' He looked up, and Abernetha saw Mrs Ramage's face glaring down from her window.

Grandpa reached into his pocket and held a black object up towards Mrs Ramage. He moved his finger and Mrs Ramage's voice rang out furiously from the black object.

'Tape recorder!' shouted Grandpa, then he grabbed Abernetha, and hurried her away through the snow.

17

'What *are* you up to, Grandpa?' asked Abernetha as they turned a corner out of Warehouse Lane.

'Maybe,' said Grandpa, peeping back round the corner into Warehouse Lane, 'Mr B Jeffries will listen to me now.'

As he peeped down the lane, he patted the recorder in his pocket; and he said, 'Is that Jennifer Antrim?'

Abernetha looked round the corner too.

Grandpa said, 'Oh. She's gone.'

'Aren't we going to see Harry? I'm hungry, Grandpa.'

'Town hall first. Then Harry. It's only half-past ten, Abernetha – not lunch time.'

'Do I have to sit in that waiting-room again?'

Abernetha sat in that waiting-room again.

She heard Mrs Ramage's voice raging out of the tape-recorder.

She heard Grandpa's voice sounding like: What do you think of that?

And she heard Mr B Jeffries' voice being jolly; then Grandpa backed out of the door, and Mr B Jeffries' hand shook Grandpa's hand.

Grandpa stomped out of the town hall.

He said, 'Oh, well,' to the snowy street.

'What did he say?' asked Abernetha. 'Is it lunch time yet?'

'Abernetha, I wanted permission to dig Miss Broom out of her grave – you know that. But Mr Jeffries didn't think the ravings of a mad old woman were enough reason. He's right, of course. We need proof.'

'I spy Angry Agatha,' said Abernetha.

And here she comes, Angry Agatha, (no anorak, having left it in Abernetha's flat) trailing through the snow, pretending she hasn't seen Abernetha and Grandpa outside the town hall.

She glances up, and seems surprised. 'Hullo,' she says, and trails past.

Grandpa sighs. He says, 'All right,' to the child's back, and she turns, looking more surprised.

Grandpa says, 'I cxpect you're hungry again, like Abernetha.'

And he leads Abernetha and Jennifer Antrim to a burger bar, where they order coke and chips, and Grandpa waits patiently over a cup of coffee.

'You didn't go home,' said Grandpa at last.

Abernetha watched Jennifer sucking her coke through a straw. The thin face said nothing.

'You followed us,' said Grandpa.

Jennifer screwed up her mouth.

Abernetha said, 'Why didn't you go to your gran? She'd have let you in out of the snow.'

'I didn't have anything to give her.'

Abernetha glanced at Grandpa for an explanation of this remark, but Grandpa only raised his eyebrows.

'And,' said Jennifer, 'she'd've told my mum I wasn't at school, so I'd've needed a belting and sent to bed.'

'Do you always give your gran something?'

'Of course. If she's going to let me get warm in her house—'

'You have to give her something?' squeaked Abernetha.

'It's only fair,' said Jennifer Antrim.

'You poor little thing!' cried Abernetha, and she really meant it. 'Do you want more chips? Another coke? You don't have to give *us* anything, does she, Grandpa?'

Grandpa was shaking his head. 'I suppose,' he said, 'you'll have to come to the hospital to see Harry. We can't send you home to a belting – however fair.'

And he stood up, looking down on Jennifer Antrim, and Abernetha could see that Grandpa's thoughts were somewhere far off. Then he shook his head, as if he didn't know what to do about his thoughts.

Then they walked out to find snow falling, and Grandpa took Abernetha's hand. And Abernetha peeped at Angry Agatha at the other side of Grandpa, and discovered that he was holding her hand too.

So they walked without speaking, all the way to Central Hospital.

18

'Who's this?' said Harry, sliding his eyes sideways through his cage at Jennifer. 'Are you Abernetha's pal?'

'Jennifer Antrim,' said Abernetha.

'Nice of you to come and see me,' said Harry.

'I want to hear the rest of the story,' said Abernetha. 'Don't eat Harry's grapes, Grandpa.'

'Sorry,' said Grandpa. 'I wouldn't mind hearing the story either, Harry – if you're up to it?'

'I've been thinking about what happened,'

said Harry, 'or what seemed to happen. It must have been a dream. Really. Yet it was so real—'

'Just tell us,' said Abernetha, and held Harry's hand.

'I fell and hurt my neck,' said Harry to Jennifer, 'and I must have been unconscious because this old woman came and led me through the snow; zooming with me through the forest. Like I said: too fast really, but everything clear and real. I kept saying, "Where are we going? Where are you taking me? Is somebody hurt? Who are you? Do I know you—?"'

Abernetha held in a sigh. Harry wasn't as good as Grandpa at telling stories."

'Then,' said Harry, 'Then – you won't believe this, Abernetha, because I don't and I was there. My feet were no longer on the ground. Still rushing through the trees we were, but above the snow. And branches didn't stop us, or tug at us, and I don't think we even disturbed the snow on the branches. A crow curved down from a Scots Pine and I swear his wing touched my shoulder but he sailed on, not noticing, shouting to other crows who were too cold, I think, to search for food.

'Then we were above the trees, and I stared at the tree tops zooming below me. I told myself I was dreaming, but no dream was ever as really, really clear. I saw a deer dart from a clearing into the forest. I saw a fox trotting with a rabbit in its mouth. I saw a buzzard circling above me, so close that I could see the gold of his eyes. And still in front of me was the old woman, dashing along, her froth of hair not in the least disturbed by the speed we were going at. Abernetha, I'm not kidding you! It must've been a dream! But really, really clear! Right, don't pull my hand off. Listen. Listen.

'We sailed higher. And I saw a train burrowing along. And maybe we flew into night, for I remember stars. Then it was daytime again, and I saw the coast, and recognised it from my school map. And the city, Abernetha, 'way below, like white Lego bricks in the snow; and cars moving. Then car lights switched on, and I saw a great cloud cast its shadow over the city. And snow began to fall.

'We dropped through the snow so that I could see nothing but snowflakes and the old woman who held onto my hand. Then something dark rushed up past me and I stopped going down, and found I was standing on the ground in the snow, and the dark something was a tree – which hadn't rushed up past me at all – I had rushed down past it.

'And I looked around at other trees. I saw gravestones, and realised I was in the cemetery. And the old woman pointed at a grave and said, "Tell your grandfather to let me out."

'And I looked at the grave, then I looked at the old woman. But she was gone. And I was pretty scared, Abernetha . . . Grandpa . . .

because it was all so real. Then I wasn't scared. I wasn't scared because I saw you, Abernetha. Though I was still muddled, because here I was in the cemetery and there you were, and the trees and the graves, and snowflakes catching up with me, beginning to fall, all as real as real, and everything seemed normal, but what about me flying over the forest and through the snow storm? That's what muddled me. But everything was all right once I saw you. So I raised my hand to wave, and you looked down at your wellies, Abernetha, then I heard your voice, and I woke up here, in the hospital and you were talking to me.'

Harry closed his eyes.

'Are you going to sleep?' asked Grandpa, and Abernetha saw that Grandpa's cheeks were pale and his eyes anxious.

She said, 'Is Harry okay? He's not worse?'

'I'm sleeping,' smiled Harry. 'Come back this evening, Abernetha.'

Harry breathed steadily; and Abernetha knew that Grandpa was anxious about Miss Broom.

Grandpa led Abernetha and Jennifer from the hospital.

They stood in the hospital doorway, peering up at the snowflakes.

Grandpa still looked anxious.

He said, 'Abernetha, I don't quite know what to do. But I must do something. We'll try Mr B Jeffries again, I think, though I doubt if he'll listen, and we'll try your grandmother, Jennifer. But if nobody listens, then I'll be forced, forced! to do something drastic, myself. And I won't like that one little bit!'

19

So they trailed, Grandpa holding Abernetha and Jennifer by the hand, through the snow again – to the town hall again, where Abernetha hung her feet from the chair in the waiting room, while Jennifer clung still to Grandpa's hand while he asked for Mr B Jeffries.

But Mr B Jeffries wasn't available, and wouldn't be available that day, or for the rest of the week. 'Or for the rest of the year,' said Grandpa. So they left the town hall, and Grandpa's face frowned more anxiously as they trudged towards Warehouse Lane.

'Are we going to see my Gran?' asked Jennifer.

'I suppose so,' grunted Grandpa. 'Though what good—'

'She'll be furious,' said Jennifer gleefully, 'because old Miss Broom isn't shut tight in her coffin. Fancy, an old woman like that flying with your Harry! You needn't look so surprised; I understood what he was talking about. And Granny Ramage'll strike you to stone for interfering, 'cos I'm going to tell her! Who'll dig *your* grave, old man?'

Jennifer snatched her hand from Grandpa's. 'You'd better dig it yourself and throw yourself in! Don't forget your five pence in the bottom of the grave! I've got your five pence! I've got your five pence!'

Abernetha and Grandpa stared in amazement as Angry Agatha went hopping away through the snow, her face as thin and nasty as ever, her fingers wiggling a coin which glinted silver in the winter daylight.

'I told you she was horrible,' said Abernetha.

'You did,' admitted Grandpa.

Grandpa stood looking after the thin dancing figure as it turned the corner into Warehouse Lane.

'I'm thinking,' said Grandpa, 'about the graves I've dug since I caught that child watching me last summer. The five-pence piece that I place in each grave was there when the coffins were lowered. If she really has a five pence from one of my graves, it can only be from Miss Broom's. Remember, Abernetha, I told you, that after Rachel filled in the grave – when I dug it out again – that I couldn't find the coin? If that child has taken it . . .'

'It's only a five pence, Grandpa.'

'Doesn't she know that money from a grave

brings only sorrow? Let's walk, Abernetha. But not towards Warehouse Lane. We can't talk to Mrs Ramage now. I do believe it's past my lunch time.'

So they turned, and almost bumped into Rachel.

‡

Rachel laughed delightedly.

'I *thought* it was you. Hello, Abernetha.' Rachel looked at Grandpa, and Abernetha thought she was going to stand on tiptoe in the snow.

Grandpa kissed Rachel on the lips. He grinned at Abernetha.

'We're going for lunch,' announced Abernetha, rather pleased that a lady wanted to kiss her Grandpa. 'I had chips and coke ages ago.'

'Half-past ten,' smiled Grandpa.

'With Angry Agatha.'

'Who?' laughed Rachel.

Grandpa said, 'Mrs Ramage's granddaughter.'

'Mrs Ramage has a family?' said Rachel.

'They live in our street,' said Abernetha. 'They're horrible.'

'I'm afraid Abernetha's right,' said Grandpa. 'Are you coming with us, Rachel? No point in going home to eat alone. Is this your lunch hour?'

'You know perfectly well . . .' began Rachel. 'Yes,' smiled Rachel. 'It's my lunch hour, Arthur. I'll come with you. But I'm paying today.'

'You've been out together before,' claimed Abernetha. 'I don't mind,' she assured them. 'I might manage another plate of chips.'

'Might you,' said Grandpa, as they walked along.

'And a sausage.'

'Really.'

Rachel took Grandpa's arm.

'And an orange juice.'

'Hm.'

Then Abernetha remembered that Rachel was paying, and she blushed.

Rachel leaned round Grandpa to look at Abernetha, and laughed her white laugh. 'No problem!' she said, and they marched into a restaurant, and ordered lunch.

As they ate, Abernetha was surprised at how amusing her Grandpa was. Oh, she knew he was fun to be with, but here was fun she'd never seen before, fun that sent Rachel into chuckles and made her put her hand on Grandpa's arm.

And Abernetha learned something during that lunch time, about her Grandpa being more than just her Grandpa, but being a man.

She learned that a woman behaves differently from a schoolgirl: that being a woman – being grown-up like Rachel – was fun; but fun with a seriousness underneath it which somehow made the fun worthwhile.

Then Abernetha noticed that Rachel's smile had faded, and that she ate while listening to Grandpa as he told her that Mr B Jeffries wasn't going to help.

'... despite Mrs Ramage ranting into the tape recorder!' grumbled Grandpa. 'How,' he demanded, 'can I get anyone to believe that your aunt is alive? You *saw* your aunt, Rachel. And I saw her behind the white stone cross the day I dug her grave. Harry flew with her to the cemetery only yesterday. Do you know what I'm saying? Harry saw her *yesterday!* And Mrs Ramage made a slip, Rachel, when she was boasting to us this morning about her revenge on Miss Broom. Did you notice, Abernetha? D'you remember me thinking things to myself and not saying anything?

'I was remembering Mrs Ramage's words: "... everyone thinks she *is* dead" when she should have said, "everyone thought she *was* dead."

'Your Auntie Broom, Rachel, is buried in my cemetery – and I believe that she's still alive!'

20

The afternoon was thinking of going to bed.

A quilt of clouds rolled over the cemetery.

As Abernetha left a trail of footprints, beginning under her kitchen window, snowflakes dropped out of the sky.

She passed the broken lump of snow which should have been the head of her snowman, without thinking about it. And ages later, she passed the tomb which had been a ship frozen in the Arctic sea, but she didn't think about that either, because she was anxious about Grandpa.

Then – after more ages – Abernetha heard a sound.

She heard the sound of metal striking earth.

Then through the falling flakes she saw a little canvas wall around the far side of Miss Broom's grave, shielding it from passersby outside the North Gate. And she saw the curve of Grandpa's bent back, inside the grave, and the flicker of his spade as earth flew into a growing heap on the white ground.

Abernetha walked forward then stood looking into the grave until Grandpa swung the spade, and his face turned up; then he straightened his back inside his old digging coat, and watched her.

'Can I help?' asked Abernetha.

'No digging for little girls,' said Grandpa gently. 'You should be at home, Abernetha.'

'Will you go to prison for digging up Miss Broom?'

'Not if she's alive,' said Grandpa. 'Maybe you *can* help, Abernetha. You know how to light my camping stove? You could put the kettle on. I'll keep working. I want to finish before dark.'

'There's snow on your back.'

'Yes,' said Grandpa, and he dug again with his long-handled spade.

Abernetha pushed open the shed door. She switched on the electric light, and closed the door quickly, because snow drifted in at her heels wanting to see what she was up to.

She used a match to light Grandpa's camping stove. His gas fire was already lit, making the shed warm. The scrape of Grandpa's spade sounded lonely in the vast cold distances of the graveyard; and Abernetha looked from the shed window, out under the arms of the beech tree which protected the shed from the snow, and she saw the dark mark of the earth heaped beside the grave, and she shivered, because she knew that Grandpa would soon have to open the coffin; and she saw too, the North Gate, and though the snow fell thickly, Abernetha – for a moment – saw four fists clutching the bars of the gate, and two faces staring in, one adult height, the other as low as a child. Then flakes pressed themselves onto the window, and Abernetha saw nothing but whiteness.

Then she remembered why she was in the shed, and filled Grandpa's kettle at the tap in the wall above the bucket that pretended to be a sink. Abernetha stood the kettle on the stove. She found mugs and the teapot and the teabags on the work bench. She touched the angel's wing which Grandpa used for sharpening his spade. Lawnmowers, she saw, and gardening tools, slept in the darkest corner of the shed, sacking keeping the lawnmowers warm.

Then Abernetha sat in Grandpa's wooden armchair with its grass-filled cushions, the cushions crackling as she put her head back.

She watched the kettle; and the scrape of the spade rang tirelessly inside her head . . .

‡

Abernetha woke. The grass cushions crackled, as she said, 'Oh,' wondering if it was time for school. Then she remembered that she was in the shed.

A burnt smell tingled her nostrils and she looked again at the kettle, and, in a sleepy way, wondered why it was twisted.

'How can the kettle be twisted?' thought Abernetha. 'And what is that smell? I mean, the kettle's made of aluminium – Oh, no!' Abernetha shook off the last of her sleep and leapt at the kettle. She snatched it off the camping stove and shrieked as the handle burnt her fingers. The kettle flew across the shed and rattled emptily against the lawnmowers. Abernetha turned on the tap and poured water over her fingers, tears sniffing in her nose. She turned off the flame on the camping stove.

Then she forgot her tears.

She listened, her face still pulled down for weeping, but really listening.

She looked out through the window. Snow blocked most of the glass, with winter's dull light beyond it. The afternoon was almost asleep.

Silence waited, except for a whispered ping from the cooling kettle, and a plip from water dripping into the bucket.

'Grandpa?' said Abernetha.

She opened the shed door.

The snow fell steadily.

No striking of metal on earth.

How could she have slept so long? Why, the kettle had been full of water, and now it was boiled dry.

She listened again, but only the snowflakes moved, falling in quiet silence, turning the ground to marshmallow, curtaining the world around the shed, so that Abernetha could see only – what had Grandpa said? – a coffin's length into the cemetery.

'Grandpa! Are you there?'

Abernetha zipped her anorak, shivering, after being asleep.

'Oh, come on, Grandpa!'

She stepped out and the snow rose almost to the tops of her wellingtons, and Abernetha stared down in fear, because here, under the sheltering beech tree, the snow had been only over her toes.

'How long have I been asleep?' she whispered. 'Grandpa?'

She ran.

'Grandpa!'

She stumbled desperately towards Miss Broom's grave. '*Grandpa!*' she screamed.

The pile of earth appeared, thick with snow. Miss Broom's gravestone stood straight, a ridiculous tower of snow balanced on its head, and the canvas wall sagged like a sail filled with a very white cloud.

Inside the grave, lumpy earth was also white.

'Grandpa?' whimpered Abernetha.

'He wouldn't leave me,' Abernetha assured herself, looking around.

'Grandpa?' She glanced again into the grave. The earth was lumpy right enough, under the snow. She saw a straight line in the earth, like the edge of something somebody had made, and she peered, and saw it was the edge of Grandpa's spade.

The spade was almost hidden in the earth and snow.

And a dreadful thought touched Abernetha.

'Grandpa?' She knelt in the snow and leaned into the grave.

The lumps which looked like earth, why, Abernetha now thought might be a man! And she gasped and leapt down into the grave, and her little hands dug through the snow, until her fingers touched soft cold cloth, and Abernetha screeched, 'Grandpa!' and dug and tugged and shook at the cloth. She dived to where Grandpa's face should be, and swept the snow aside, and—

'GRANDPA!'

—for there was his face, blue and frozen, snow in his eyes, his mouth open enough to let Abernetha glimpse a cold smile – but Grandpa wasn't smiling.

He wasn't doing anything.

21

Snow descended onto Abernetha. Snowflakes landed on Grandpa's face and did not melt.

But Abernetha took no time to think about this. She grabbed Grandpa's head and shook it. She rubbed his cheeks with her hands. She bounced her knees on his chest because she knew his heart had to be started, and maybe bouncing would start it! And she grabbed his nose to shut his nostrils, and put her mouth over Grandpa's mouth and blew her warm breath into him! And something touched her back.

Something landed on her back, gently, and lay there, firm, clinging perhaps to her anorak, and horrors crept over Abernetha's skin, and she wanted to scream but dared not even move; dared not even breathe life into Grandpa—

Then the thing slipped, and beside Abernetha, Grandpa's arm dropped, and she realised that the thing on her back had been his hand; and his eyes moved and his mouth breathed, and his breath said, 'Help me.'

And she helped him.

Abernetha pulled his head up. She clambered over his head, so that it was in her lap. She pushed his shoulders to raise them, and Grandpa's arms shifted, and together they sat him up.

'Rub my back,' gasped Grandpa. 'Harder! Harder than that! Hit it! Hit my back! Beat my back! Oh, I feel that! You're getting the circulation going, Abernetha. Enough! Enough. That's my good girl. I must get to the shed. Help me stand. I'll lean on you. Okay. My legs are numb with cold. I'm standing. That's it. I can hold onto the sides of the grave. I don't know how I'm going to get out. Hit my legs, Abernetha. Up and down. Pinch them. That's it. Is the shed warm? Good. How am I going to get out of this grave?'

'Wave your arms, Grandpa!'

'Yes. There we go. I've never been so cold. Did you breathe into me, Abernetha? An angel's kiss, that was. I hadn't actually stopped breathing, but you put warmth into me, child. You did the right thing. You woke me up. That evil old woman. Oh, that wicked child! To think we had her in our house . . .'

'What do you mean?' cried Abernetha, ceasing her pummelling of Grandpa's legs while she looked up into his face.

The blueness had gone, though his hair was white with snow.

'Mrs Ramage, of course,' gasped Grandpa. 'I must get into the shed, Abernetha. Push me up. And your Angry Agatha. Get behind me and push me up! I've got my elbows on the ground! Oh! That's it!'

Then Grandpa's weight went off Abernetha's shoulder and he disappeared upwards. Then his arm came down and lifted Abernetha as if she weighed nothing, and Abernetha knew that Grandpa's strength had returned, and that not much was wrong with him now.

They went into the shed and closed the door, and Grandpa jumped up and down and waved his arms mightily, and he smelled of earth and coldness; and he asked Abernetha where the tea was.

So she filled the kettle and put it back on the camping stove's flame, and she explained to Grandpa why the kettle was twisted, but he only said, 'Good thing it didn't get a hole burnt in its bottom.'

Then they drank tea which tasted of burnt metal, and for a while Grandpa shivered monstrously in the armchair, but the tea warmed him, and his jumping about had warmed him, and – fortunately – his clothes had been too cold to melt the snow much, so he wasn't wet through; only his old digging coat steamed a little in front of the gas fire.

'Came out of the snow like ghosts,' said Grandpa, as he clutched his mug.

'I thought they really were ghosts for a second. I was taking a breather, you see. I was close to uncovering the coffin, Abernetha, so I needed a breather to steady my nerves. Oh, I do have nerves.

'I know, I know. I'm the bravest, strongest person in the world, but I do have nerves; and opening a coffin is not a happy thing to do, especially when I just might go to jail for doing it! Phew. Well, I'm warmer now, thank goodness. And thank you, Abernetha. Saved my life, you did. What? Oh, Mrs Ramage?

'Yes. She and that child came out of the snow while I was having my breather. Standing on the coffin, I was, Abernetha, only my head was above ground level, and that foul great woman came raging towards me—'

'So I did see them!' said Abernetha, remembering the fists on the bars of the North Gate. And she explained this to Grandpa.

And he nodded. 'Taking the child home, I expect,' he said. 'They would pass the North Gate, going to Jennifer's end of our street. So they saw my canvas wall around the grave—'

'They must have heard you digging.'

'They knew, well enough what I was doing, I guess,' sighed Grandpa. 'Then you dozed off in this heat. They'd take quite a time to go round to the West Gate and come to the grave . . .

'Well. She came raging out of the snow, her fists hanging like cannon balls, her feet beating the snow flat, and that child was standing back, its mouth open as if it might laugh; and the woman was saying, "I'll have my revenge! Open this grave would you?

and show me up! Well, I know just how to hurt you!"

'Abernetha,' said Grandpa, 'I thought she was going to kick my head because she was still striding towards me, and I got ready to duck. But she stopped, the toes of her boots level with my mouth, and she bent over me, her eyes like bits of coal, and before I could move, Abernetha, her fist came out of nowhere and caught me such a blow on the side of the head.

'She may have hit me again – I don't know. My legs felt like paper because there was no strength in them. The daylight faded though I think my eyes were still open. I heard myself fall with a slightly hollow sound onto the coffin which was just underneath the earth; but I didn't feel myself landing. I could still hear her voice.

She was saying something about making things even. That life should be fair. That no one had treated her fairly when she was a girl. That everything landed on *her* shoulders and her just a child; having to carry coal up four flights of stairs to feed the range. And she had to black-lead the range. You know what a range is, Abernetha? one of these old-fashioned black iron fireplaces with a built-in oven, that took up half a wall in a tenement house. Oh, I don't remember everything she said, but she certainly was angry with her parents, and she had made up her mind – oh, I remember – made up her mind that her life, when she grew up, would be fair.

'I couldn't answer her. I was gasping. I couldn't see. I felt snowflakes gathering on my cheeks, but I couldn't turn my face away. I thought she was going to bury me on top of Miss Broom.

'But she had stopped talking. Or I couldn't hear her any more. And I grew colder. I thought of shouting for you, Abernetha, but I wasn't sure that I could, and I wasn't sure if that Ramage woman had left. She didn't know you were in the shed, of course, and I couldn't risk letting her know, by calling.'

Grandpa sat.

Abernetha saw that he was thinking.

He said, 'She said she knew just how to hurt me.'

'She hit you,' said Abernetha.

Grandpa shook his head. 'She hit me for fun. She knew,' he murmured, 'just how to hurt me. Did she mean you, Abernetha? Would she hurt you, to hurt me?'

Grandpa's face relaxed in dismay.

'What's the time?' he demanded.

'I don't know. What's wrong, Grandpa? I'm safe here with you! Mum's at work and Harry's in hospital—'

'Rachel!' whispered Grandpa. 'Rachel lives in the flat underneath. She's an easy target, Abernetha. If it's after five o'clock she'll be home—'

Grandpa rose out of the armchair. He pushed his tea mug at Abernetha.

'Grandpa,' said Abernetha, 'what about Miss Broom?'

Grandpa hesitated.

He said, 'Rachel first. Then Miss Broom. Come on, Abernetha. I can't leave you here. Come on, child. Outside! Out! Out! We have to run! Or my Rachel may die!'

22

But they couldn't run, Abernetha and Grandpa. They couldn't run to save Rachel, not all the way to the West Gate through snow which was as deep as Grandpa's shins even in the shelter of the beech tree, and up to Grandpa's knees no doubt, beyond the tree.

So they hesitated, standing outside the shed, Grandpa turning this way and that, talking desperately, thinking out loud to Abernetha about how to reach Rachel quickly. Then he stumbled into the shed and returned carrying a pickaxe. 'For breaking up frozen ground, Abernetha!' he cried. 'But not today! This way!' And he strode through the snow, peering into the white veil of flakes, towards Miss Broom's grave.

Abernetha wanted to ask why they were heading for the grave. Weren't they going to save Rachel first, like he'd said? After all, Miss Broom had been buried for months—

But Grandpa hurried past the grave.

Snowflakes made Abernetha blink as she followed Grandpa. Branches of bare trees fingered her clothing as if to say, 'Are you warm enough, Abernetha?'

Then the North Gate, chained shut these fifty years, barred Abernetha's way.

Beyond the gate, people hurried home from work, heads down against the snow, and car drivers leaned close to their windscreens as they drove into the white dusk; so no one noticed as Abernetha and Grandpa loomed from the depths of the graveyard; no one noticed Grandpa slip the point of the pickaxe behind the chain which secured the North

Gate, and as a bus roared slowly along, no one heard the chain snap with a *bang!* as Grandpa's strength proved too much for the chain's old steel links.

Then: 'Help me!' said Grandpa, and he gripped the gate and pulled. And Abernetha gripped and pulled, but she felt her little strength was doing nothing. She might as well try to pull the tenement down, she thought.

Under the snow, the gate was rooted in weeds. A sycamore, as thick in its body as Grandpa, grew only inches away from the gate. No way could anybody open this gate. Not even Mr B Jeffries if he brought a bulldozer from the town hall – could open this gate. Not even Desperate Dan—

The gate moved.

'Pull!' gasped Grandpa.

The gate groaned.

The snow around the foot of the gate split, and weeds tore. The gate touched the sycamore, and still Grandpa pulled, and Abernetha felt her eyes open in astonishment for the gate continued to open, and she looked at where the metal was against the sycamore, and her mouth gaped when she saw that the metal was bent, and it was bending more as Grandpa pulled.

Then he stopped pulling, and said, 'That's wide enough.' And he squeezed through the opening and dashed out onto the pavement, leaving Abernetha to follow.

Then Grandpa's hand landed on her shoulder, and Abernetha found herself in a taxi.

Then they were out of the taxi, a few streets away, in Warehouse Lane, Grandpa's thumb on the buzzer beside Rachel's name.

'I should have asked the taxi-driver if it was after five o'clock!' groaned Grandpa.

'She's not answering.'

'I know!' snarled Grandpa. 'Sorry, Abernetha.'

'Here she comes!' cried Abernetha, and

she waved along the pavement, where, under the street lights, Rachel was smiling and waving back.

Then Rachel's face tipped upwards, her eyes narrowed against the snowflakes, and Abernetha looked up, and above her was the glow of Mrs Ramage's window, and in the glow, leaned the shape of the old woman's head and beefy shoulders.

'Mrs Ramage,' breathed Abernetha, and Grandpa looked.

He said, 'Nothing she can do, not now that Rachel's here with us.'

But he didn't sound sure.

'Hello, you two,' said Rachel, huddling close, and smiling and searching her handbag.

She unlocked the door. 'Let's get in out of this weather.'

They crowded in, and Grandpa shut the door, and they took a step towards the stairs which would take them up one flight to Rachel's flat.

But they didn't get onto the stairs.

Half-way down the flight stood Mrs Ramage.

Behind her sneered the thin face of Angry Agatha.

And in Mrs Ramage's face was a look of dreadful, utter fury.

23

'Forget it,' said Grandpa, and Abernetha thought his voice shook just ever so slightly. 'Forget your wickedness, Mrs Ramage,' said Grandpa. 'It does you no good. You can't hurt me – or mine.' And his hands touched Abernetha and Rachel on the shoulder.

'Knowing our names was no use to you. You haven't succeeded in piling your evil thoughts around us. Give it up, old woman.'

Mrs Ramage stumped down a step.

Abernetha thought that Mrs Ramage was going to speak, for she looked at Grandpa; but her eyes turned their fury on Abernetha and

Rachel; and she stumped down again; another step, and another; then fairly ran down to meet Grandpa—

Oh, not to meet him!

To beat him with her fists!

Her fists swung with blinding swiftness. Abernetha found herself bumped back against the outside door by Grandpa as he dodged. She glimpsed Rachel darting past Mrs Ramage to give Grandpa more space, but the old woman snarled and swung a backhand blow that caught Grandpa's raised arm, but still had weight enough to send him staggering; and the old woman bounded at Rachel, who shrieked and fled past the stairs, and flung open a door which led into the white falling darkness behind the building.

Rachel ran into the snow.

Mrs Ramage ran after her.

Angry Agatha stood on the stairs, cackling

that Granny had brought her back here to celebrate them getting revenge, and now their revenge was really starting!

But Grandpa ignored her and dashed after Mrs Ramage, and Abernetha – after one look at Angry Agatha (which must have been a terrible look, because the thin child stopped cackling) – after one look, Abernetha ran after Grandpa into the knee-deep snow.

She could see nothing but white falling darkness.

She knew she was in Rachel's back garden.

She had seen the back garden before, from Mrs Ramage's window, and she remembered that it wasn't really a garden, but a long grassy slope which leaned down towards the whisky river.

Someone staggered out of the snow towards her, and Abernetha cried, 'Rachel! Where's Mrs Ramage? Where's Grandpa? Grandpa!' she screamed. 'Rachel's here! Grandpa!'

Rachel held Abernetha. 'Is he coming?' she panted.

They listened.

'I can hear the river,' whispered Abernetha.

'It's very full with all this snow. Can you see anything?'

Something moved behind the dropping flakes, and Mrs Ramage stomped out of the darkness, glaring, her great shoulders already white.

Her glare turned into a grin.

'Grandpa's here with us!' cried Abernetha, hoping Grandpa would hurry.

'No he's not,' puffed Mrs Ramage. 'He's lying down.' She grinned more and raised one fist. 'Lying down. It's your turn to lie down,' she told Rachel and Abernetha. 'No one makes a fool of Maisie Ramage.'

She stepped high through the snow towards them.

'Life must be fair. Everybody knows that.'

She shouted suddenly, 'Life must be fair!'

And she lunged forward, making Abernetha and Rachel step away. But Mrs Ramage lunged again, and her fist swung, striking Rachel on the shoulder.

Then she struck at Abernetha, and the blow thudded like a drum on Abernetha's chest. The sound of it seemed to linger through Abernetha's body, echoing down to her toes as if her legs were hollow, then rolling upwards to fill her head with its noise. And Abernetha found herself lying in the snow, but almost – really – sitting up, because the snow was as deep as an armchair; and she realised she could see further into the darkness.

Light from the open door behind her – the door to the stairs – spread far down the white slope to the river. Lights beyond the river shone on foam as water frothed on the rocks, though Abernetha could not see the rocks in the darkness, nor the smoother flowing water. Abernetha told herself that the snow had stopped falling, which was why she could see. It had stopped very suddenly, she said to herself. Had she been knocked out for a minute by Mrs Ramage?

And where was Rachel? And Grandpa?

'Grandpa!' she yelled, and something touched her arm, which was Rachel crouching beside her.

Rachel pointed and Abernetha turned her head, and she realised that she was seeing as if she was looking down a tunnel; she could not see out the corners of her eyes, which was why she had not seen Rachel beside her.

Then her eyes cleared, and she saw properly where Rachel was pointing, and she stared as Grandpa – light from the doorway shining as yellow as paint down one side of him, his hand holding his head – faced Mrs Ramage.

Grandpa held his free hand palm-out to Mrs Ramage as if to calm her, and he spoke soothingly, but Mrs Ramage stood raging, her fists striking but not reaching Grandpa. And she staggered closer to him though the snow was round her thighs, and Grandpa stepped back still talking; but he did not strike at the old woman; he did not raise his fist though Mrs Ramage swept her mighty blows left and right, not stopping, not resting, utterly determined to hurt and hurt and hurt again; and Abernetha suddenly felt sorry that anyone should be so full of anger.

Then she noticed Jennifer Antrim, standing close to the building, watching, her face dull; tears, thought Abernetha, shining in the dark, on her cheeks.

Then a roar of rage made Abernetha look again at Mrs Ramage. The old woman raised both arms. Her fury boiled in her face as the yellow light from the door turned her into a demon – and she flung herself at Grandpa as if in a last desperate attempt to destroy him.

Her fists descended. Grandpa's upraised palm pushed them aside.

He stepped back and sat in the snow.

The sweep of Mrs Ramage's fists unbalanced her. The whirl of her arms turned her round. She fell onto her side and rolled down the slope flattening the snow with her tremendous weight.

Snow stuck to her clothes.

Abernetha remembered pushing a snowball in the cemetery until it was big enough to reach her knees.

Mrs Ramage rolled faster. She cried out.

Grandpa sat up straight.

More snow wrapped itself around her body, leaving bare grass in a trail behind her.

Grandpa stood up.

'Help!' squawked Mrs Ramage.

But no one moved.

Further she rolled – that wicked old woman – further down the slope, whirling towards the whisky river; and bigger she grew with snow; and still no one moved as she vanished – a gigantic human snowball – into the darkness near the water; then a splash reached Abernetha, and she saw white lumps in the river catching the distant lights, and the lumps melted and dissolved until there were no more lumps; and the water foamed, and the darkness was dark.

‡

Rachel was speaking as Abernetha sat in the snow, stunned by Mrs Ramage disappearing.

'What?'

'We can't just leave her!' said Rachel again, and Abernetha knew she was talking to Grandpa.

'You can't leave her!' cried Rachel.

Grandpa's head moved, as if he had wakened from a daze. He stepped onto the trail of bare grass and jogged along it down the slope.

'Can you get up, Abernetha?' cried Rachel.

Abernetha's chest ached where Mrs Ramage

had hit her, but her head was clear. And she followed Rachel down the bare grass, and stood with Rachel and Grandpa on the bank of the whisky river.

'Do you see her?' asked Rachel.

'The lights are in my eyes,' said Abernetha. 'And it's so dark in the water. I see something there. Among the rocks. Won't she be swept away by now? Oh, I hope not! Grandpa, I think that's her! Did you hear a cry?'

But before Abernetha could think, Grandpa put one hand on the grass, and leapt feet-first into the river.

'Arthur!'

The river surged around Grandpa's middle. He reached back and caught Rachel's hand, steadying himself.

'Once I'm on the rocks,' he shouted, 'I'll be okay!' He let go Rachel's hand, and walked as if on a tight-rope. He became a black shadow against the lights. He was a hero, striding to save the life of someone who hated him, because it was the right thing to do.

And suddenly, he became a giant because he had stepped up onto a rock and the water snarled only around his ankles. Then he said, 'Wait,' loudly enough for Abernetha to hear; and he moved further over the rocks, then he bent, and became a rock himself.

A gasp reached Abernetha and Rachel, and Grandpa stood up, the fat bulk of Mrs Ramage clinging to him, and he returned across the rocks, and lowered Mrs Ramage into the deep water at the river's edge, and he passed her to Rachel and Abernetha. Then Grandpa was in the deep water, and, with a shout and a mighty heave from Grandpa, Mrs Ramage landed on the bank, gasping and weeping.

Abernetha looked around for Angry Agatha, but she could not see the child anywhere.

And Mrs Ramage – lying in the snow beside the whisky river – was shuddering with cold.

Grandpa, too, was shuddering.

He said, 'Rachel, give Abernetha your key. Abernetha, get up to the flat and put all the heating on. Find something warm to wrap us in. Get moving, child!'

Abernetha got moving.

She lit Rachel's gas fire with a match, and turned the central heating up full, glad that it was similar to the central heating at home.

She felt embarrassed searching Rachel's rooms, but she found duvets, and stacked them in the sitting-room at the fire to warm.

Then she ran to the kitchen and poured milk into a pan, lit the gas, and looked for drinking chocolate.

And while she made the chocolate, she heard Grandpa and Rachel bringing Mrs Ramage into the house. And Abernetha found herself crying.

She heard Rachel telling Grandpa to get

out of his wet clothes – she would undress Mrs Ramage.

So Abernetha continued crying while the milk squirmed with heat.

Then she felt better, and rinsed her face at the sink, poured the chocolate into mugs and took it through to the fire, where she found Mrs Ramage sitting on the floor huddled inside a tent of duvets, her face white like a fat cheese; and Rachel humped in a chair exhausted.

Then Grandpa came in wearing his weekend clothes, and Abernetha frowned at him, as if to say: 'How come your weekend clothes are here?' But Grandpa only grabbed his hot chocolate, and said, 'I have to get back to the graveyard, Rachel. I have to make sure – one way or another – about Auntie Broom.'

And Mrs Ramage said, 'You'd better hurry, old man. You'd better dig her up quickly, because I couldn't hold on to my wicked thoughts after you saved me from the river.

Hurry,' urged Mrs Ramage, 'because her heart's beating again, and she needs to be warm; and she's breathing and I don't know how much air is in that coffin—'

In the midst of this talk, Grandpa was suddenly gone, his mug rocking on its side on the carpet, steam from his chocolate rising from the pile; and Rachel stared after him as the door banged, and Grandpa's feet sounded on the stairs.

24

Oh, later, what happened at the cemetery became part of Grandpa's story.

He told it to Mum and Harry and Abernetha over and over. How he ran through the snowy streets, all the way to the North Gate, and squeezed through the gap, thanking Goodness that the snow still wasn't falling so that he could see his way. And he ran in the dents his and Abernetha's feet had made in the snow earlier – to the shed, and grabbed a screwdriver. Then he raced to the grave and jumped inside, his feet banging hollowly on the coffin. And how he heard panting inside the coffin, as if someone was short of breath; and he swept snow and earth aside with his palms and placed the screwdriver into the head of a screw-nail which held the lid shut and he turned the screw; then he turned another, but the gasping grew faint so that he knew he didn't have time to loosen all the screws, so he rammed the screwdriver under the lid, eased it open enough to get his fingers in, then tore it clean off.

And the old lady sighed. She champed her lips. Grandpa sat her up and lifted her out of the grave. He carried her to the shed and sat her in the grassy-cushioned armchair close to the blast of the gas heater; he wrapped her in sacking off the lawnmowers. He made tea, and fed her a biscuit. And he listened in amazement when she said (eventually) oh, wasn't it lucky she was buried for only a few minutes! Though she had dreamed a dreadful dream that she'd been buried for months! How very kind of you to dig me up so quickly! And she had no memory whatever! of haunting Rachel or anyone else. Then Grandpa slipped away when it seemed she was all right, and found a taxi. And the taxi entered the cemetery by the West Gate, *bump-bumping* bravely through the snow, right to the shed door, and Auntie Broom went in comfort to hospital.

And that was a relief!

Abernetha, of course (while showing-off where her fingers had been burnt by the kettle), had to add her part of the story, so that Grandpa could tell it all together, and her part was waiting in Rachel's flat with Mrs Ramage inside her tent of duvets, and poor Rachel, whiter than the snow outside with worry, listening for Grandpa's return.

And when the doorbell rang, Rachel shrieked, for they hadn't heard Grandpa's feet on the stairs, and when Abernetha and Rachel opened the door, they found Angry Agatha numb with cold, numb with shame, and numb with hunger, hoping to be let in.

Angry Agatha held out her hand to Abernetha.

'What?' said Abernetha.

'It's your grandfather's five-pence piece.'

'Is it,' said Abernetha, not taking the coin.

'You'd better come in,' said Rachel.

'And we'll feed you,' said Abernetha. 'Won't we, Rachel?'

'Of course.'

'And warm you.'

'That's right,' said Rachel.

'And forgive you,' said Abernetha sternly.

'Yes,' said Rachel.

'We'll even give you back your schoolbag and your anorak,' said Abernetha, pulling Jennifer into the sitting-room, 'which you left in our flat. And to really, really be good to you – to make you feel really, really, *really* guilty and rotten – we'll also give you back your granny.'

Mrs Ramage looked round from inside the duvets.

Jennifer said, 'I thought she was drowned. I thought she was drowned, and I ran away. You saved her? Your grandfather saved her?'

She sank onto a chair. 'You do things for each other, don't you? I don't understand. That's not fair. Doing things isn't fair. I don't understand. I can't understand.'

And she closed the five-pence piece in her hand, and sat in silence for a long, long, long time.

Another Hodder Children's book

STRANGE HOTEL

Hugh Scott

Buried in a sea of pines, the hotel stands lonely.
No one sunbathes on the lawn.
No one sits at the tables.
The drive lies silent, like a grey snake.

Suddenly a dove flutters.
Ian senses something is wrong.
Is he making a mistake entering the hotel?
And who are the people inside?
Are they real, or are they creatures from a dream?
For Ian Oaktake, this is the holiday which changes his world.

Another Hodder Children's book

NIGHT PEOPLE

Maggie Pearson

Jools and her father are always on the move. Until they reach a town where Chas has a past, and where he'd like his daughter to have a future.

While Chas plays his beloved jazz, Jools explores the strange world into which they have stepped. A world of night people. Until one by one the murders start. Sinister forces are unleashed, but does Jools know where real danger lies?

Another Hodder Children's book

GHOST CHAMBER

CELIA REES

He had seen inside the mysterious casket.
Now, no one must know of its existence.
He smoothed the wall he had just completed
and began to work, shaping and placing,
stone on stone, walling himself in. Alive.

The dark secret of the mysterious Templar Knight stays hidden for over five hundred years – until the Goodman family move into *The Saracen's Head* – an old pub with a haunted past. A secret lies waiting to be unearthed. A ghost who must not be disturbed...

ORDER FORM

0 340 68332 5	STRANGE HOTEL *Hugh Scott*	£3.99 ☐
0 340 65572 0	OWL LIGHT *Maggie Pearson*	£3.99 ☐
0 340 68076 8	NIGHT PEOPLE *Maggie Pearson*	£3.99 ☐
0 340 69371 1	THE BLOODING *Patricia Windsor*	£3.99 ☐
0 340 68300 7	COMPANIONS OF THE NIGHT *Vivian Vande Velde*	£3.99 ☐
0 340 68656 1	LOOK FOR ME BY MOONLIGHT *Mary Downing Hahn*	£3.99 ☐

All Hodder Children's books are available at your local bookshop or newsagent, o can be ordered direct from the publisher. Just tick the titles you want and fill i the form below. Prices and availability subject to change without notice.

Hodder Children's Books, Cash Sales Department, Bookpoint, 39 Milton Park Abingdon, OXON, OX14 4TD, UK. If you have a credit card you may orde by telephone – (01235) 831700.

Please enclose a cheque or postal order made payable to Bookpoint Ltd to th value of the cover price and allow the following for postage and packing:
UK & BFPO – £1.00 for the first book, 50p for the second book, and 30p for each additional book ordered up to a maximum charge of £3.00.
OVERSEAS & EIRE – £2.00 for the first book, £1.00 for the second book and 50p for each additional book.

Name..

Address..

....

....

If you would prefer to pay by credit card, please complete:
Please debit my Visa/Access/Diner's Card/American Express (delete a applicable) card no:

Signature..

ExpiryDate..